1755-1794 Florian, Charles Yeld

Florian's Fables

Selected and Edited for the use of Schools by Charles Yeld

1755-1794 Florian, Charles Yeld

Florian's Fables
Selected and Edited for the use of Schools by Charles Yeld

ISBN/EAN: 9783744772594

Printed in Europe, USA, Canada, Australia, Japan

Cover: Foto ©Andreas Hilbeck / pixelio.de

More available books at **www.hansebooks.com**

FLORIAN'S FABLES

SELECTED AND EDITED FOR THE USE OF SCHOOLS

BY THE

REV. CHARLES YELD, M.A.

ST. JOHN'S COLLEGE, CAMBRIDGE

HEADMASTER OF UNIVERSITY SCHOOL, NOTTINGHAM

WITH PHILOLOGICAL AND EXPLANATORY NOTES,

EXERCISES, DIALOGUES, AND VOCABULARY

ILLUSTRATED

London

MACMILLAN AND CO.

AND NEW YORK

1888

CONTENTS

INTRODUCTION

TWENTY years ago, to nine boys (and more than one master) out of every ten it would have been quite a revelation to have had pointed out to them that French is only Latin popularised and made simple in a conquered Province. But since the eminent labours of M. Brachet have been made accessible to English readers, there has been a great change for the better in the teaching of French, and no good teacher now would dream of ignoring the history of the language if his pupils possessed any knowledge at all of Latin. I am convinced that no boy or girl who has learned the Latin Accidence ought to be allowed to learn French without being taught something of its history, and of the steps by which the Latin words which he finds in his *Cæsar*, or *Phædrus*, or *Livy* have been brought to their present French form. Nor need there be any difficulty in teaching even young boys this much, as I hope to point out here.

To understand the language intelligently, he must

have put before him something of the gradual and methodical process of change by which the French of our day has grown to be what it is. As M. Brachet says : "Present usage depends on ancient usage, and can only be explained by it : modern French without Old French is a tree without roots ; Old French by itself a tree without branches or leaves ; the separation of the two is an injustice to both ;" and equally an injustice is it to make orphans of both by separating them from their common Parent Latin. The main difficulty which so long stood in the way of this historical teaching of French was the want of anything like a text-book intelligible to boys, and within reasonable compass of size and price. Sixty years ago Raynouard (1761-1836), the "Father of Romance Philology," of whom Schlegel says (*Kritische Schriften*, vol. i. p. 356) that he did more for the history of the French language than all the academicians of his country, published a series of works upon the history and grammar of the "Romance languages" (by which name are commonly understood French, Italian, Spanish and its twin sister Portuguese, Wallachian, the Provençal *patois*, and the dialects of the Grisons) ; but they were little known in England until Sir George Cornewall Lewis in his *Essay on the Romance Languages* refuted them with remarkable learning and ability ; and they were altogether too voluminous to be of any use to young students. His theory was that the *Romance Languages*, formed from the corruption of classical Latin, were common to all the countries of Europe in which Latin had been spoken, and are preserved in a *pure form* in the poetry of the Troubadours (*Grammaire de la Langue Romane*, pp. 5, 6)—a regular fixed language, with rules of construction, etc., understood throughout the Roman Europe. This was the *common source* from which the various Romance dialects were formed: from this, by slightly different modifications, came French, Italian, Spanish, etc.

This theory, which had been put forward as a conjecture by Smollett (*Travels in France and Italy*, letter xxi.), and was adopted by Perticari in Italy, has been proved to be a mistake—"an excusable mistake, however, in the time of Raynouard, as nearly all the documents on which modern researches and modern theories are based were then unpublished, or published in a very mutilated form" (Meissner, *Palæstra Gallica*, p. 2). By means of these documents, which are for the most part inscriptions, oaths, or legal deeds, modern scholars have proved, without possibility of question now, that the Romance languages are merely a continuation of the Latin *popularly spoken*. Among the most eminent of these scholars are Sir G. C. Lewis, whose *Essay* (London, 1835) I have just referred to, Professor Diez, whose *Grammatik der Romanischen Sprachen* (Bonn, 1836-

1844) shows great learning and research; Burguy, *Grammaire de la Langue d'Oil* (Berlin, 1853); Littré, whose *Dictionary* is a prodigious and quite invaluable monument of his literary labours and critical acumen; and M. Brachet, whose *Historical Grammar of the French Tongue*, admirably translated by Dr. Kitchin, Dean of Winchester, has become the standard text-book on French philology in all our public schools, and is one of the most interesting and even amusing schoolbooks that have been published during this century.

It is well known to scholars that in the third century B.C. Plautus, the comic poet (B.C. 254-184), and Ennius (B.C. 239-169), introduced certain popular mistakes into their poetry—as, for example, the forms *collus* and *dorsus* for the neuter words *collum* and *dorsum*, etc. —and that in Cæsar's time there existed a wide difference between the *Sermo Nobilis*, the literary, aristocratic, classical Latin, and the soldier's talk, the *Verbum Castrense*. "The latter," says M. Brachet (*Historical Grammar*, p. 5), "was unwritten, and we might have remained ignorant of its existence had not the Roman grammarians revealed it to us by exhorting their students to avoid, as low and trivial, certain expressions which, they tell us, were in common vulgar use." As late as the second century A.D. the popular dialect was still in the shade, literary Latin shone with great brilliancy;

schools of law and of oratory had been established in all the Roman colonies, and not the least famous were those of Gaul, who had won for herself an eminence to which Juvenal bears witness when he styles her the Nursery of Pleaders. But literary Latin, fixed by Livius Andronicus, and Cato, and Lucretius, polished by Cicero and others, was the dialect of the patricians —" the language of a restricted class, of a political party, of a literary set" (Max Müller, *Science of Language*, p. 56). It was the language of the cultured portion of the population of Latium, and in Latium of Rome itself. But when the colonies began to dispute the supremacy of Latium in matters political, the literary supremacy was disputed too. The " free and enlightened " colonist flung off the fetters of literary accuracy : he altered the words to suit his enfranchised tastes, and introduced others which had hitherto been considered unfit for polite society. In time these became recognised as words to be allowed, even though objectionable ; and insensibly they came to be used by patrician and plebeian alike. One might hint at a parallel which seems to exist in the revolt of the American colonies from the sovereignty of Britain, and the effect of this revolt upon the American dialect : more startling in some respects than the change from classical Latin to Old French. Hundreds of words have been invented and have found a home in America, which are, to say

the least, extraordinary. Every one knows the *strong
preterites* in the stanza—

> "As stealthily to steal he stole,
>   His chink he softly chunk ;
> And many a leary smile he smole,
> -   And many a wink he wunk."

It is to be hoped they may never be used otherwise
than by way of joke—to show what *Red Republicanism
in letters* will condescend to : but remembering by what
subtle and unperceived stages of attachment words
worm themselves into the diction and grammar of a
language, one cannot help wondering what the American
dialects will grow to, under the liberty of invention and
alteration which every American citizen claims as his
heritage in literature as in all else. The " Queen's
English " may some day become almost as unintelligible
to our American cousin as the Carlovingian Latin is to
the modern Parisian.

I should like to indicate here a mere outline which
would, I think, be sufficient for a teacher to give to his
or her young pupils, but which could be added to as a
larger mastery of Latin should make more extended
instruction intelligible, and allow of M. Brachet's
Grammar being used as the text-book.

Let first the two distinct sets of words be pointed
out : a few examples would be sufficient illustration,
such as—

Sermo Nobilis.	Verbum Castrense.	French.	English.
caput	testa	tête	head.
equus	caballus	cheval	horse.
felis	catus	chat	cat.
os	bucca	bouche	mouth.
urbs	villa	ville	city.

While the *Sermo Nobilis* was spoken in Gaul down to the Fall of the Roman Empire, it was being gradually supplanted by the *Verbum Castrense*, which eventually took its place altogether.

In the changes made, until classical words became popular Latin, and ultimately French, the most important were—

The reduction of the genders to Two, *Masculine* and *Feminine;* the *Neuter* gender disappearing altogether;

The reduction of the *Six* Cases to Two, *Nominative* and *Accusative.* But even these were more than the mass of people cared to distinguish one from the other, and soon they were

Further reduced to One, the *Accusative.*

This will help the pupil to remember, because he will quite understand *why*, that the *Plural* of French nouns and adjectives always ends in *s* or an equivalent *x* or *z*.

Singular.	Plural.
catum	catos.
testam	testas.

A further shortening brought the words to *chat, chats, tête, têtes,* etc.

It will not be beyond the power of even little boys to grasp the three Rules which M. Brachet lays down as invariable in all words that have been changed naturally by the popular voice and ear. Call these *Popular* words (adopting M. Brachet's terms, so that when they come to use his text-book they will be familiar with its terminology), as distinct from the words brought into the language straight from the Latin by the Savans of the fifteenth and sixteenth centuries and called *Learned* words.

Three simple and easily learned Rules :—

1. The Latin accent is always kept in words of *Popular* origin, and generally *not in Learned words.* Point out that in Latin the accent, " the *soul* of a word," falls upon *the last syllable but one,* if that syllable be *long* (as in *amáre*), but if it be short, then on the *last but two* (as in *ángelus*). Illustrate with—

Latin.	Popular French.	Learned French.
débitum	détte	debít.
exámen	essáim	examén.
móbilis	méuble	mobíle.
pórticus	pórche	portíque.

2. The second Rule is that " the short *unaccented* vowel, which directly precedes the accented syllable, always disappears in French words of *Popular* origin,

being always preserved in *Learned* words." Give examples—

Latin.	Popular Word.	Learned Word.
blasph(ĕ)máre	blâmer	blasphémer.
hosp(ĭ)tále	hôtel	hôpital.
nav(ĭ)gáre	nagér	naviguer.
sim(ŭ)láre	semblér	simuler.

3. The third Rule refers to the consonants ; to the loss of the *medial* consonant, *i.e.* a consonant standing between two vowels, like the *t* in *dotare :* M. Brachet's Rule is : "All French words which drop the *medial consonant* are *popular* in origin ; words of *learned* origin retain it."

Latin.	Popular Word.	Learned Word.
Au(g)ústus	Août	auguste.
cre(d)éntia	créance	credence.
re(g)ális	royal	regale.
repli(c)áre	replier	repliquer.

These are the three chief Rules : fairly mastered, they give an insight into French philology which must lead any intelligent pupil to further study.

One other Rule should be added to complete what may be regarded as essential for any young student to know and understand.

4. A *short* vowel in the last syllable, or last syllable but one, always disappears (or in the last syllable is replaced by *e* not pronounced).

Latin.	French.
tábŭlam	table.
orácŭlum	oracle.
pósĭtum	poste.
víncĕre	vaincre.

I speak from experience when I say that with this knowledge as a foundation, boys will themselves build upon it, will ask questions in doing either Latin or French in order to get at the connexion which they can partly see for themselves. They have been provided with two sets of puzzles, and will be so interested in solving them that the French lesson will become a real pleasure, instead of being, as it so often has been and is, a mere drudgery.

It is in order to give boys a greater interest in their French work as well as to further the accurate knowledge of French, and to encourage philological study, that I have prepared this little book. I only ask that this Introduction may be made a first stage in reading it, and that the slight historical sketch I have given may be thoroughly mastered before the reading of the Fables is entered upon. Two or three lessons will suffice to accomplish this, and when once accomplished I am certain that both teachers and pupils will find greater interest in the lesson, and the dry bones of French grammar will be clothed upon with a form of beauty that will delight both the learner and the teacher.

Beyond this, I am hopeful that they will all thank me for having introduced to them, with English help, such amusing and beautiful Fables.

C. Y.

I

THE TWO TRAVELLERS

Two men are travelling together on foot. One of them finds a purse of gold which he will not share with his friend. Presently they are attacked by robbers, and the friend escapes leaving his companion to be robbed of the purse and its contents.

LES DEUX VOYAGEURS

Le compère Thomas et son ami Lubin
Allaient à pied tous deux à la ville prochaine.
   Thomas trouve sur son chemin
   Une bourse de louis pleine ;
Il l'empoche aussitôt. Lubin, d'un air content,   5
   Lui dit : " Pour nous la bonne aubaine ! "
—" Non," répond Thomas froidement :
" *Pour nous* n'est pas bien dit ; *pour moi*, c'est différent."
Lubin ne souffle plus : mais, en quittant la plaine,
Ils trouvent des voleurs cachés au bois voisin.   10
   Thomas tremblant, et non sans cause,
Dit : " Nous sommes perdus ! "—" Non," lui répond Lubin.
" *Nous* n'est pas le vrai mot ; mais *toi*, c'est autre chose."
Cela dit, il s'échappe à travers les taillis.
   Œ   B

Immobile de peur, Thomas est bientôt pris ;   15
   Il tire la bourse et la donne.

Qui ne songe qu'à soi quand la fortune est bonne,
   Dans le malheur n'a point d'amis.

II

THE MOLE AND THE RABBITS

We often know our defects ; we do not always acknowledge them.

Some rabbits in a flowery mead are playing at Blind-man's-buff. The poor "blind-man" is likely to be "blind-man" till morning, for, while the other rabbits dance and leap around him and pull his ears and tail, he can't catch one. A mole underground, hearing the noise overhead, comes out, and, being blind, is caught immediately. She insists on being blindfolded in her turn, for she was caught in fair play. They cannot tie the bandage tight enough, however ; for, tie it as they will, she still can see, she says.

LA TAUPE ET LES LAPINS

Chacun de nous souvent connaît bien ses défauts,
   En convenir, c'est autre chose :
On aime mieux souffrir de véritables maux,
   Que d'avouer qu'ils en sont cause.
   Je me souviens, à ce sujet,   5
   D'avoir été témoin d'un fait
Fort étonnant et difficile à croire ;
   Mais je l'ai vu : voici l'histoire.

   Près d'un bois, le soir, à l'écart,
   Dans une superbe prairie,   10
Des lapins s'amusaient, sur l'herbette fleurie,
   A jouer au colin-maillard.

Des lapins ! direz-vous, la chose est impossible.

Rien n'est plus vrai pourtant : une feuille flexible

Sur les yeux de l'un d'eux en bandeau s'appliquait,   15

    Et puis sous le cou se nouait.

    Un instant en faisait l'affaire.

Celui que ce ruban privait de la lumière

Se plaçait au milieu ; les autres alentour
     Sautaient, dansaient, faisaient merveilles,   20
     S'éloignaient, venaient tour à tour
     Tirer sa queue ou ses oreilles.
Le pauvre aveugle alors, se retournant soudain,
Sans craindre pot au noir, jette au hasard la patte,
     Mais la troupe échappe à la hâte,   25
Il ne prend que du vent, il se tourmente en vain,
     Il y sera jusqu'à demain.
     Une taupe assez étourdie,
     Qui sous terre entendit ce bruit,
     Sort aussitôt de son réduit   30
     Et se mêle dans la partie
     Vous jugez que, n'y voyant pas,
     Elle fut prise au premier pas.
" Messieurs," dit un lapin, " ce serait conscience,
Et la justice veut qu'à notre pauvre sœur   35
     Nous fassions un peu de faveur ;
     Elle est sans yeux et sans défense ;
Ainsi je suis d'avis. . . ."—" Non," répond avec feu
La taupe, "je suis prise, et prise de bon jeu ;
Mettez-moi le bandeau."—" Très-volontiers, ma chère ; 40
Le voici : mais je crois qu'il n'est pas nécessaire
     Que nous serrions le nœud bien fort."
—" Pardonnez-moi, monsieur," reprit-elle en colère,
" Serrez bien, car j'y vois. . . . Serrez, j'y vois encor."

III

THE NIGHTINGALE AND THE PRINCE

A young prince, taking a walk with his tutor, sees a nightingale singing exquisitely in a tree close by. He wants to catch and cage it ; so to keep its song. But he only frightens it away into the wood. He complains that, while his court is filled with stupid sparrows who give him no pleasure, he cannot keep the nightingale which has charmed him. His tutor explains that stupid people push themselves forward ; true worth must be sought.

LE ROSSIGNOL ET LE PRINCE

Un jeune prince, avec son gouverneur
    Se promenait dans un bocage,
    Et s'ennuyait, suivant l'usage,
    C'est le profit de la grandeur.
    Un rossignol chantait sous le feuillage :   5
Le prince l'aperçoit et le trouve charmant ;
Et, comme il était prince, il veut, dans le moment,
    L'attraper et le mettre en cage.
    Mais pour le prendre il fait du bruit,
    Et l'oiseau fuit.   10
" Pourquoi donc," dit alors Son Altesse en colère,
    " Le plus aimable des oiseaux
Se tient-il dans les bois, farouche et solitaire,
Tandis que mon palais est rempli de moineaux ?"
    " C'est," lui dit le Mentor, " afin de vous instruire 15
    De ce qu'un jour vous devez éprouver :
    Les sots savent tous se produire ;
Le mérite se cache, il faut l'aller trouver."

IV

THE BLIND MAN AND THE CRIPPLE

We ought to help each other. Two wretched men, one blind, the other crippled and helpless, are so wearied with the burdens of life that they ask to die. But the blind man stumbles accidentally on the lame, and proposes that they shall join company and help each other. He will carry the cripple, who in turn will guide his steps; so they will bear each other's burdens.

L'AVEUGLE ET LE PARALYTIQUE

Aidons-nous mutuellement,
La charge des malheurs en sera plus légère ;
 Le bien que l'on fait à son frère
Pour le mal que l'on souffre est un soulagement.
Confucius l'a dit ; suivons tous sa doctrine.   5
Pour la persuader aux peuples de la Chine,
 Il leur contait le trait suivant.

 Dans une ville de l'Asie
 Il existait deux malheureux,
L'un perclus, l'autre aveugle, et pauvres tous les deux. 10
Ils demandaient au ciel de terminer leur vie :
 Mais leurs cris étaient superflus,
Ils ne pouvaient mourir. Notre paralytique,
Couché sur un grabat dans la place publique,
Souffrait sans être plaint ; il en souffrait bien plus. 15
 L'aveugle, à qui tout pouvait nuire,
 Était sans guide, sans soutien,
 Sans avoir même un pauvre chien
 Pour l'aimer et pour le conduire.

Un certain jour, il arriva 20
Que l'aveugle, à tâtons, au détour d'une rue,
Près du malade se trouva ;
Il entendit ses cris, son âme en fut émue.
Il n'est tel que les malheureux
Pour se plaindre les uns les autres. 25
" J'ai mes maux," lui dit-il, "et vous avez les vôtres :
Unissons-les, mon frère, ils seront moins affreux."
—"Hélas !" dit le perclus, "vous ignorez, mon frère,
Que je ne puis faire un seul pas ;
Vous-même vous n'y voyez pas : 30
A quoi nous servirait d'unir notre misère ?"
—"A quoi ?" répond l'aveugle ; "écoutez : à nous deux
Nous possédons le bien à chacun nécessaire :
J'ai des jambes, et vous des yeux.
Moi, je vais vous porter ; vous, vous serez mon guide : 35
Vos yeux dirigeront mes pas mal assurés ;
Mes jambes, à leur tour, iront ou vous voudrez.
Ainsi, sans que jamais notre amitié décide
Qui de nous deux remplit le plus utile emploi,
Je marcherai pour vous, vous y verrez pour moi." 40

V

THE MOTHER, THE CHILD, AND THE OPOSSUM

A child, seated on his mother's knee, asks about the opossum
which he sees, with its young, upon the heath. The mother
describes the animal as one gifted with great tenderness and
affection for its little ones, and as aided in its care of them by
being provided with a pouch, into which they can jump when-
ever danger approaches. The surest place of safety is in a
mother's breast.

La Mère, l'Enfant, et les Sarigues

" Maman," disait un jour à la plus tendre mère
Un enfant péruvien sur ses genoux assis,
" Quel est cet animal qui, dans cette bruyère,

Se promène avec ses petits ?
Il ressemble au renard."—"Mon fils," répondit-elle,   5
"Du sarigue c'est la femelle.
Nulle mère pour ses enfants
N'eut jamais plus d'amour, plus de soins vigilants.
La nature a voulu seconder sa tendresse,
    Et lui fit près de l'estomac   10
Une poche profonde, une espèce de sac,
    Où ses petits, quand un danger les presse,
    Vont mettre à couvert leur faiblesse.
Fais du bruit, tu verras ce qu'ils vont devenir."
L'enfant frappe des mains ; la sarigue attentive   15
    Se dresse, et, d'une voix plaintive,
Jette un cri : les petits aussitôt d'accourir,
    Et de s'élancer vers la mère,
En cherchant dans son sein leur retraite ordinaire.
    La poche s'ouvre, les petit   20
    En un moment y sont blottis ;
Ils disparaissent tous : la mère avec vitesse
    S'enfuit emportant sa richesse.
La Péruvienne alors dit à l'enfant surpris
    "Si jamais le sort t'est contraire,   25
Souviens-toi du sarigue, imite-le, mon fils :
L'asile le plus sûr est le sein d'une mère."

VI

The Old Tree and the Gardener

A gardener is about to cut down an old pear-tree that used to bear fruit largely, but now has none. At the first stroke of his axe the tree pleads for longer life, reminding him of the fruit it used to yield. But the gardener wants wood, he says. Then a hundred nightingales plead for the boughs in which they sing and charm away his wife's lonely weariness. He gives another stroke. Then a swarm of bees fly out and remind him how they make their honeycomb in the trunk, and here is gain for him. So he spares the tree, from self-interest, not from gratitude.

Le Vieux Arbre et le Jardinier

Un jardinier, dans son jardin,
　　Avait un vieux arbre stérile ; .
C'était un grand poirier, qui jadis fut fertile :
Mais il avait vieilli, tel est notre destin.
Le jardinier ingrat veut l'abattre un matin ;　　　　5
　　Le voilà qui prend sa cognée.
　　Au premier coup l'arbre lui dit :
" Respecte mon grand âge, et souviens-toi du fruit
　　Que je t'ai donné chaque année.
La mort va me saisir, je n'ai plus qu'un instant ;　　10
　　N'assassine pas un mourant
Qui fut ton bienfaiteur."—"Je te coupe avec peine,"
Répond le jardinier ; "mais j'ai besoin de bois."
　　Alors, gazouillant à la fois,
　　De rossignols une centaine　　　　　　　　　　15
S'écrie : "Epargne-le, nous n'avons plus que lui.
Lorsque ta femme vient s'asseoir sous son ombrage,
Nous la réjouissons par notre doux ramage ;

Elle est seule souvent, nous charmons son ennui."
Le jardinier les chasse et rit de leur requête ;   20
Il frappe un second coup.   D'abeilles un essaim
Sort aussitôt du tronc, en lui disant : "Arrête,
  Ecoute-nous, homme inhumain :
  Si tu nous laisses cet asile,
  Chaque jour nous te donnerons   25
Un miel délicieux, dont tu peux à la ville
  Porter et vendre les rayons ;
Cela te touche-t-il ?"—"J'en pleure de tendresse,"
  Répond l'avare jardinier :
"Eh! que ne dois-je pas à ce pauvre poirier   30
  Qui m'a nourri dans sa jeunesse ?
Ma femme quelquefois vient ouïr ces oiseaux ;
C'en est assez pour moi : qu'ils chantent en repos.
Et vous, qui daignerez augmenter mon aisance,
Je veux pour vous de fleurs semer tout ce canton."   35
Cela dit, il s'en va, sûr de sa récompense,
  Et laisse vivre le vieux tronc.
  Comptez sur la reconnaissance,
  Quand l'intérêt vous en répond.

VII

The Peacock, the two Goslings, and the Diver

A peacock, admired by the other birds as he spreads his
brilliant tail, is abused by two goslings who notice only his
crooked legs, flat feet, and shrill cry.   A diver suddenly comes
out of the marsh and tells them they are quite right about the
peacock ; but *their* legs are more crooked, *their* feet flatter
than his, *their* cackling more disagreeable than his shrill note,
and they will never have his tail.

Le Paon, les deux Oisons, et le Plongeon

Un paon faisait la roue, et les autres oiseaux
    Admiraient son brillant plumage.
Deux oisons nasillards du fond d'un marécage
    Ne remarquaient que ses défauts.

" Regarde," disait l'un, " comme sa jambe est faite,   5
    Comme ses pieds sont plats, hideux !"
—" Et son cri," disait l'autre, " est si mélodieux,
    Qu'il fait fuir jusqu'à la chouette !"
Chacun riait alors du mal qu'il avait dit.

    Tout à coup un plongeon sortit :   10
" Messieurs," leur cria-t-il, " vous voyez d'une lieue
Ce qui manque à ce paon : c'est bien voir, j'en conviens;
Mais votre chant, vos pieds, sont plus laids que les siens,
    Et vous n'aurez jamais sa queue."

VIII

The Child and the Mirror

    A child, who has been brought up in a poor village, returns to his parents' home, and is surprised at finding a mirror there. At first he admires himself in it; then makes a face at the glass, and is very angry that it does the same at him. He strikes it, and hurts his hands. This makes him worse, and he stands before the mirror crying, and beating it, until his mother comes and shows him that it is all his own doing. If he will smile, it will smile back. The world, she tells him, will treat him as he treats it.

L'Enfant et le Miroir

Un enfant élevé dans un pauvre village
Revint chez ses parents, et fut surpris d'y voir
    Un miroir.
    D'abord il aima son image ;
Et puis, par un travers bien digne d'un enfant,   5
    Et même d'un être plus grand,
    Il veut outrager ce qu'il aime,

Lui fait une grimace, et le miroir la rend.

Alors son dépit est extrême :

Il lui montre un poing menaçant ; 10

Il se voit menacé de même.

Notre marmot fâché s'en vient, en frémissant,

Battre cette image insolente ;

Il se fait mal aux mains. Sa colère en augmente ;

Et, furieux, au désespoir, 15

Le voilà, devant ce miroir,

Criant, pleurant, frappant la glace.

Sa mère, qui survient, le console, l'embrasse,

Tarit ses pleurs, et doucement lui dit :

" N'as-tu pas commencé par faire la grimace 20

A ce méchant enfant qui cause ton dépit ?

—" Oui."—" Regarde à présent : tu souris, il sourit ;

Tu tends vers lui les bras, il te les tend de même ;

Tu n'es plus en colère, il ne se fâche plus.

De la société tu vois ici l'emblême : 25

Le bien, le mal, nous sont rendus."

IX

THE CRICKET

A cricket, hidden in the grass, is watching a butterfly of brilliant colours fluttering from flower to flower, and complains that he himself has nothing to make him admired—talent, shape, colour—nothing that any one will care for or even notice. As well not live ! There comes a troop of children : with hats and caps they chase and catch the pretty butterfly, and between them pull him to pieces. The cricket is no longer vexed : his retired life is happiest after all.

Le Grillon

Un pauvre petit grillon
  Caché dans l'herbe fleurie,
Regardait un papillon
  Voltigeant dans la prairie.
L'insecte ailé brillait des plus vives couleurs.   5
L'azur, le pourpre et l'or éclataient sur ses ailes.

Jeune, beau, petit-maître, il court de fleurs en fleurs,
Prenant et quittant les plus belles.
  "Ah!" disait le grillon, "que son sort et le mien
    Sont différents! Dame nature   10
    Pour lui fit tout, et pour moi rien.
Je n'ai point de talent, encor moins de figure ;
Nul ne prend garde à moi, l'on m'ignore ici-bas !
    Autant vaudrait n'exister pas."
    Comme il parlait, dans la prairie   15
    Arrive une troupe d'enfants.
    Aussitôt les voilà courants
Après ce papillon dont ils ont tous envie.
Chapeaux, mouchoirs, bonnets, servent à l'attraper.
L'insecte vainement cherche à leur échapper,   20
    Il devient bientôt leur conquête.
L'un le saisit par l'aile, un autre par le corps ;
Un troisième survient, et le prend par la tête :
    Il ne fallait pas tant d'efforts
    Pour déchirer la pauvre bête.   25
"Oh, oh!" dit le grillon, "je ne suis plus fâché ;
Il en coûte trop cher pour briller dans le monde.
Combien je vais aimer ma retraite profonde !"
    Pour vivre heureux, vivons caché.

X

THE ROPE-DANCER AND THE BALANCING-POLE

An acrobat upon a tight-rope is doing feats of skill. With his balancing-pole in his hands he runs up and down, to the admiration of the many spectators. But why carry this heavy pole? he asks himself; he would be much more light and springy without it; so he throws it away, and at once begins to waver—holds out both his hands—falls—and breaks his nose—while everybody laughs. Virtue, reason, law, authority, are the balancing-poles of life.

LE DANSEUR DE CORDE ET LE BALANCIER

Sur la corde tendue un jeune voltigeur
Apprenait à danser ; et déjà son adresse,
    Ses tours de force, de souplesse,
    Faisaient venir maint spectateur.
Sur son étroit chemin on le voit qui s'avance,   5
Le balancier en main, l'air libre, le corps droit
    Hardi, léger autant qu'adroit ;
Il s'élève, descend, va, vient, plus haut s'élance,
    Retombe, remonte en cadence,
    Et, semblable à certains oiseaux   10
Qui rasent en volant la surface des eaux,
    Son pied touche, sans qu'on le voie,
A la corde qui plie et dans l'air le renvoie.
Notre jeune danseur, tout fier de son talent,
Dit un jour : " A quoi bon ce balancier pesant   15
    Qui me fatigue et m'embarrasse ?
Si je dansais sans lui, j'aurais bien plus de grâce,
    De force et de légèreté."

C

Aussitôt fait que dit.   Le balancier jeté,
Notre étourdi chancelle, étend les bras et tombe.   20
Il se casse le nez, et tout le monde rit.

Jeunes gens, jeunes gens, ne vous a-t-on pas dit
Que sans règle et sans frein tôt ou tard on succombe ?
La vertu, la raison, les lois, l'autorité,
Dans vos désirs fougueux vous causent quelque peine.   25
      C'est le balancier qui vous gêne,
      Mais qui fait votre sûreté.

XI

The Viper and the Leech

A viper complains to a leech that they are very differently
treated by men, and he very unjustly ; for, while they both bite
alike, and make the same wound, men kill him, but let the leech
take as much blood from them as he cares to do.   The leech
replies that there is really a very great difference in their bites,
for the viper kills, while he cures, men.

La Vipère et la Sangsue

La vipère disait un jour à la sangsue :
   " Que notre sort est différent !
On vous cherche ; on me fuit : si l'on peut on me tue,
      Et vous, aussitôt qu'on vous prend,
      Loin de craindre votre blessure,   5
      L'homme vous donne de son sang
      Une ample et bonne nourriture :
Cependant vous et moi faisons même piqûre."
      La citoyenne de l'étang
      Répond : "Oh ! que nenni, ma chère ;   10

La vôtre fait du mal, la mienne est salutaire.
Par moi plus d'un malade obtient sa guérison ;
Par vous tout homme sain trouve une mort cruelle.
Entre nous deux, je crois, la différence est belle :
  Je suis remède et vous poison."   15

  Cette fable aisément s'explique
  C'est la satire et la critique.

XII

The Miser and his Son

A miser one day, to give himself a treat, bought some apples which he carefully locked up and kept, only eating them as they got rotten. His son discovered the treasure, and, with two school-friends, got into the storeroom and had a good feast. As they are finishing off the apples, the miserly old father catches them, and cries out wofully for his fruit. His son tells him he need not mind, for they have only eaten what he would not eat—the *good apples!*

L'Avare et son Fils

Par je ne sais quelle aventure,
Un avare, un beau jour, voulant se bien traiter,
    Au marché courut acheter
    Des pommes pour sa nourriture.
    Dans son armoire il les porta,   5
    Les compta, rangea, recompta,
Ferma les doubles tours de sa double serrure,
    Et chaque jour les visita.
    Ce malheureux, dans sa folie,
    Les bonnes pommes ménageait;   10
Mais, lorsqu'il en trouvait quelqu'une de pourrie,
    En soupirant il la mangeait.
Son fils, jeune écolier, faisant fort maigre chère,
Découvrit à la fin les pommes de son père.
Il attrape les clefs et va dans ce réduit,   15
Suivi de deux amis d'excellent appétit.
Or vous pouvez juger le dégât qu'ils y firent,
    Et combien de pommes périrent!
    L'avare arrive en ce moment,

De douleur, d'effroi palpitant :   20
"Mes pommes!" criait-il: "coquins, il faut les rendre,
Ou je vais tous vous faire pendre."
—"Mon père," dit le fils, " calmez-vous, s'il vous plaît ;
Nous sommes d'honnêtes personnes :
Et quel tort vous avons-nous fait ?   25
Nous n'avons mangé que les bonnes."

XIII

THE CAT AND THE RATS

A cat, daintily fed, has grown too lazy to trouble about catching the rats. They, in their turn, have grown bold, and, by the ill advice of one orator among them, they agree no longer to eat grain and bread, but only *cats*. They accordingly form themselves into an army, with Mr. Orator for their general, and attack the sleeping Angora. Pussy wakes up and quickly lays them in the dust. Two escape, and philosophise in their hiding-place—"One loses one's fair share when one tries to get everything."

LE CHAT ET LES RATS

Un angora, que sa maîtresse
Nourrissait de mets délicats,
Ne faisait plus la guerre aux rats ;
Et les rats, connaissant sa bonté, sa paresse,
Allaient, trottaient partout, et ne se gênaient pas.   5
Un jour, dans un grenier retiré, solitaire,
Où notre chat dormait après un bon festin,
Plusieurs rats viennent dans le grain
Prendre leur repas ordinaire.
L'angora ne bougeait. Alors mes étourdis   10
Pensent qu'ils lui font peur ; l'orateur de la troupe

Parle des chats avec mépris.
On applaudit fort, on s'attroupe,
On le proclame général.
Grimpé sur un boisseau qui sert de tribunal   15
" Braves amis," dit-il, " courons à la vengeance.
De ce grain désormais nous devons être las ;
Jurons de ne manger désormais que des chats ;

On les dit excellents ; nous en ferons bombance.

A ces mots, partageant son belliqueux transport,   20
Chaque nouveau guerrier sur l'angora s'élance,
  Et réveille le chat qui dort.
Celui-ci, comme on croit, dans sa juste colère,
  Couche bientôt sur la poussière
  Général, tribuns et soldats.   25
  Il ne s'échappa que deux rats,
Qui disaient, en fuyant bien vite à leur tanière :
  " Il ne faut point pousser à bout
  L'ennemi le plus débonnaire.
On perd ce que l'on tient quand on veut gagner tout."   30

XIV

The Mirror of Truth

In the Golden Age Truth moved among men, showing them in her mirror their true selves. But, when men became wicked in the later days, Truth fled to the skies, throwing her mirror to the earth and breaking it to pieces. Since then men have sought for the pieces, but each seeker has found only a fragment.

Le Miroir de la Vérité

Dans le beau siècle d'or, quand les premiers humains,
  Au milieu d'une paix profonde,
  Coulaient des jours purs et sereins,
  La Vérité courait le monde
  Avec son miroir dans les mains.   5
Chacun s'y regardait, et le miroir sincère
Retraçait à chacun son plus secret désir,
  Sans jamais le faire rougir :

Temps heureux, qui ne dura guère !
L'homme devint bientôt méchant et criminel ;   10
   La Vérité s'enfuit au ciel
En jetant de dépit son miroir sur la terre ;
   Le pauvre miroir se cassa.
Ses débris, qu'au hasard la chute dispersa,
   Furent perdus pour le vulgaire.   15
Plusieurs siècles après on en connut le prix ;
Et c'est depuis ce temps que l'on voit plus d'un sage
   Chercher avec soin ces débris,
Les retrouver parfois ; mais ils sont si petits,
   Que personne n'en fait usage.   20
   Hélas ! le sage le premier
   Ne s'y voit jamais tout entier.

XV

THE BULLFINCH AND THE RAVEN

A bullfinch and a raven live in the same house ; the one delighting everybody by his sweet singing, the other making himself a constant nuisance by croaking for bread, cheese, anything he can see, which they give him to stop his cries. The poor bullfinch, whose song disturbs no one, is forgotten, neglected, and one morning found dead—of hunger. The raven goes on worrying everybody, and gets all he asks for.

LE BOUVREUIL ET LE CORBEAU

Un bouvreuil, un corbeau, chacun dans une cage,
   Habitaient un même logis.
   L'un enchantait par son ramage
La femme, le mari, les gens, tout le ménage ;
L'autre les fatiguait sans cesse de ses cris ;   5

Il demandait du pain, du rôti, du fromage,
    Qu'on se pressait de lui porter,
    Afin qu'il voulût bien se taire.
Le timide bouvreuil ne faisait que chanter,
Et ne demandait rien : aussi, pour l'ordinaire,   10
    On l'oubliait ; le pauvre oiseau
    Manquait souvent de grain et d'eau.
Ceux qui louaient le plus de son chant l'harmonie

N'auraient pas fait le moindre pas
Pour voir si l'auge était remplie.   15
Ils l'aimaient bien pourtant, mais ils n'y pensaient pas.
Un jour on le trouva mort de faim dans sa cage.
"Ah! quel malheur!" dit-on : "las! il chantait si bien!
De quoi donc est-il mort? Certes, c'est grand dommage!"
Le corbeau crie encore et ne manque de rien.   20

XVI

THE LION AND THE LEOPARD

A lion, king of a great plain, covets the possessions of his
neighbour the leopard, but is hindered from making a raid on
them by fear of the bears and panthers who live between his
territory and the leopard's. He sends an old fox to the leopard
as his ambassador, to propose an alliance. They are to be Lords
Supreme ; whoever will not bow to them must die. The treaty
being concluded, they quickly eat up the bears and panthers,
and the lion, easily finding a cause of quarrel, comes to blows
with the leopard and kills him.

LE LION ET LE LÉOPARD

Un valeureux lion, roi d'une immense plaine,
Désirait de la terre une plus grande part,
Et voulait conquérir une forêt prochaine,
        Héritage d'un léopard.
L'attaquer n'était pas chose bien difficile ;   5
Mais le lion craignait les panthères, les ours,
Qui se trouvaient placés juste entre les deux cours.
Voici comment s'y prit notre monarque habile
Au jeune léopard, sous prétexte d'honneur,
        Il députe un ambassadeur ;   10
C'était un vieux renard. Admis à l'audience,

Du jeune roi d'abord il vante la prudence,
Son amour pour la paix, sa bonté, sa douceur,
        Sa justice et sa bienfaisance ;
Puis, au nom du lion, propose une alliance   15
        Pour exterminer tout voisin
        Qui méconnaîtra leur puissance.
Le léopard accepte ; et, dès le lendemain,
        Nos deux héros, sur leurs frontières,

Mangent, à qui mieux mieux, les ours et les panthères. 20
Cela fut bientôt fait ; mais, quand les rois amis,
    Partageant le pays conquis,
    Fixèrent leurs bornes nouvelles,
    Il s'éleva quelques querelles :
Le léopard lésé se plaignit du lion ;   .   25
    Celui-ci montra sa denture
    Pour prouver qu'il avait raison.
Bref, on en vint aux coups. La fin de l'aventure
    Fut le trépas du léopard :
    Il apprit alors, un peu tard,   30
Que contre les lions les meilleures barrières
Sont les petits Etats des ours et des panthères.

XVII

The Monkey who shows the Magic-Lantern

An entertainer has, in addition to the attractions of his magic-lantern, a monkey which by its tricks and cleverness greatly amuses his audience. One fête-day he is away, and the monkey takes the opportunity of inviting his friends—dogs, cats, turkeys, little pigs — to his magic-lantern entertainment. He makes them a great speech, then shows the lantern—the sun, the moon, Adam and Eve, the animals, "Did you ever see anything equal to it ?" he exclaims. They are all dreadfully puzzled ; they can't see anything but the blank wall ! but they don't like to say so. At last the cat exclaims she "can see nothing." The monkey continues, however, his eloquent explanation, but to little purpose, for *he has forgotten to light up the lantern !*

Le Singe qui montre la Lanterne Magique

Messieurs les beaux esprits, dont la prose et les vers
Sont d'un style pompeux et toujours admirable,

Mais que l'on n'entend point, écoutez cette fable,
Et tâchez de devenir clairs.

Un homme qui montrait la lanterne magique   5
    Avait un singe dont les tours
    Attiraient chez lui grand concours.
Jacqueau, c'était son nom, sur la corde élastique
    Dansait et voltigeait au mieux,
    Puis faisait le saut périlleux,   10
Et puis sur un cordon, sans que rien le soutienne,
    Le corps droit, fixe, d'aplomb,
    Notre Jacqueau fait tout du long
    L'exercice à la prussienne.
Un jour qu'au cabaret son maître était resté   15
    (C'était, je pense, un jour de fête),
    Notre singe en liberté
    Veut faire un coup de sa tête.
Il s'en va rassembler les divers animaux
    Qu'il peut rencontrer dans la ville :   20
    Chiens, chats, poulets, dindons, pourceaux,
    Arrivent bientôt à la file.
" Entrez, entrez, messieurs," criait notre Jacqueau ;
" C'est ici, c'est ici qu'un spectacle nouveau
Vous charmera gratis. Oui, messieurs, à la porte   25
On ne prend point d'argent, je fais tout pour l'honneur."
    A ces mots, chaque spectateur
    Va se placer, et l'on apporte
La lanterne magique ; on ferme les volets ;
    Et, par un discours fait exprès,   30
    Jacqueau prépare l'auditoire.

Ce morceau vraiment oratoire
Fit bâiller ; mais on applaudit.
Content de son succès, notre singe saisit
    Un verre peint qu'il met dans sa lanterne.   35
        Il sait comment on le gouverne,
Et crie en le poussant : "Est-il rien de pareil ?
        Messieurs, vous voyez le soleil,
        Ses rayons et toute sa gloire.
Voici présentement la lune ; et puis l'histoire   40
    D'Adam, d'Eve et des animaux . . .
        Voyez, messieurs, comme ils sont beaux !
        Voyez la naissance du monde ;
Voyez . . ." Les spectateurs, dans une nuit profonde,
Écarquillaient leurs yeux et ne pouvaient rien voir :   45
    L'appartement, le mur, tout était noir.
"Ma foi," disait un chat, "de toutes les merveilles
        Dont il étourdit nos oreilles,
        Le fait est que je ne vois rien."
        —"Ni moi non plus," disait un chien.   50
"Moi," disait un dindon, "je vois bien quelque chose ;
        Mais je ne sais pour quelle cause
        Je ne distingue pas très-bien."
Pendant tous ces discours, le Cicéron moderne
Parlait éloquemment et ne se lassait point.   55
        Il n'avait oublié qu'un point :
        C'était d'éclairer sa lanterne.

XVIII

THE LINNET

A young linnet, an only son, is quite "spoiled" by his mother, who pampers him exceedingly. He grows up conceited and disagreeable, quizzes all the other birds, and makes himself objectionable all round. His mother mildly suggests that he shall be a little modest; they cannot help recognising his great qualities, but he might pretend a little not to know that he has them. But, by advice of an old blackbird, he goes off to the woods to see something of the world, and be educated. He there begins by chaffing a woodpecker, and suffers for it; a magpie teaches him a further lesson, and he returns at length to his mother gentle, modest, and refined. Adversity is an invaluable teacher.

LE LINOT

Une linotte avait un fils
Qu'elle adorait selon l'usage ;
C'était l'unique fruit du plus doux mariage,
Et le plus beau linot qui fût dans le pays.
Sa mère en était folle, et tous les témoignages   5
Que peuvent inventer la tendresse et l'amour
Etaient pour cet enfant épuisés chaque jour.
Notre jeune linot, fier de ces avantages,
Se croyait un phénix, prenait l'air suffisant,
     Tranchait du petit important   10
     Avec les oiseaux de son âge,
Persiflait la mésange ou bien le roitelet,
     Donnait à chacun son paquet,
Et se faisait haïr de tout le voisinage.
Sa mère lui disait : "Mon cher fils, sois plus sage,   15
Plus modeste surtout.   Hélas ! je conçois bien
Les dons, les qualités qui furent ton partage ;
     Mais feignons de n'en savoir rien,
     Pour qu'on les aime davantage."
     A tout cela notre linot   20
     Répondait par quelque bon mot.
La mère en gémissait dans le fond de son âme.
     Un vieux merle, ami de la dame,
Lui dit : "Laissez aller votre fils au grand bois ;
     Je vous réponds qu'avant un mois   25
Il sera sans défauts." Vous jugez des alarmes
De la mère, qui pleure et frémit du danger ;
Mais le jeune linot brûlait de voyager :

Il partit donc malgré ses larmes.

A peine est-il dans la forêt, 30

Que notre petit personnage

Du pivert entend le ramage,

Et se moque de son fausset.

Le pivert, qui prit mal cette plaisanterie,

Vient à bons coups de bec plumer le persifleur, 35

Et, deux jours après, une pie

Le dégoûte à jamais du métier de railleur.

Il lui restait encore la vanité secrète

De se croire excellent chanteur ;

Le rossignol et la fauvette 40

Le guérirent de son erreur.

Bref, il retourna chez sa mère,

Doux, poli, modeste et charmant.

Ainsi l'adversité fit dans un seul moment

Ce que tant de leçons n'avaient jamais pu faire. 45

XIX

The Monkeys and the Leopard

Some monkeys in a wood are having a good romp. The young Prince Leopard hears the noise, and comes from his lair to see what they are doing. They are all terrified at the sight of him, but he assures them that he is friendly, and not at all proud, and would like to join their game. They are astonished at his condescension, and welcome him ; but each time that in their merry sport he strikes one of them, his claws tear the skin and draw blood. One by one they make excuse to leave the game, and get away as quickly as they can.

Les Singes et le Léopard

Des singes dans un bois jouaient à la main chaude ;

Certaine guenon mauricaude,

Assise gravement, tenait sur ses genoux
La tête de celui qui, courbant son échine,
  Sur sa main recevait les coups.   5
  On frappait fort, et puis devine !
Il ne devinait point ; c'étaient alors des ris,
  Des sauts, des gambades, des cris.
Attiré par le bruit du fond de sa tannière,
Un jeune léopard, prince assez débonnaire, 10
Se présente au milieu de nos singes joyeux.

Tout tremble à son aspect. " Continuez vos jeux,"
Leur dit le léopard, " je n'en veux à personne :
   Rassurez-vous, j'ai l'âme bonne ;
Et je viens même ici, comme particulier,   15
   A vos plaisirs m'associer.
   Jouons, je suis de la partie."
   —" Ah ! monseigneur, quelle bonté !
Quoi ! Votre Altesse veut, quittant sa dignité,
Descendre jusqu'à nous !"—" Oui, c'est ma fantaisie   20
Mon Altesse eut toujours de la philosophie,
    Et sait que tous les animaux
      Sont égaux.
Jouons donc, mes amis, jouons, je vous en prie."
Les singes enchantés crurent à ce discours,   25
    Comme l'on y croira toujours.
    Toute la troupe joviale
Se remet à jouer : l'un d'entre eux tend la main ;
    Le léopard frappe, et soudain
On voit couler du sang sous la griffe royale.   30
Le singe cette fois devina qui frappait ;
    Mais il s'en alla sans le dire,
   Ses compagnons faisaient semblant de rire,
    Et le léopard seul riait.
Bientôt chacun s'excuse et s'échappe à la hâte,   35
    En se disant entre leurs dents :
    " Ne jouons point avec les grands,
Le plus doux a toujours des griffes à la patte."

XX

The Children and the Partridges

A farmer's two children, somewhat "spoiled" by their indulgent father, looking for birds' nests one day, find a partridge's with thirteen little ones in it. They chase the little birds, and catch six each, but so quarrel over the thirteenth that at last the elder boy throws the disputed bird at his brother's head. The younger boy flings back one of his six, and has another thrown at him, and so they go on until all thirteen are lying dead on the ground, and their father coming up reproves them for their wicked quarrelling, which has led to such cruelty.

Les Enfants et les Perdreaux

Deux enfants d'un fermier, gentils, espiègles, beaux,
  Mais un peu gâtés par leur père,
  Cherchant des nids dans leur enclos,
  Trouvèrent de petits perdreaux
  Qui voletaient après leur mère.   5
Vous jugez de leur joie, et comment mes bambins
  A la troupe qui s'éparpille
  Vont partout couper les chemins,
  Et n'ont pas assez de leurs mains
  Pour prendre la pauvre famille !   10
La perdrix, traînant l'aile, appelant ses petits,
  Tourne en vain, voltige, s'approche ;
  Déjà mes jeunes étourdis
  Ont toute sa couvée en poche.
Ils veulent partager, comme de bons amis.   15
Chacun en garde six ; il en reste un treizième :
  L'aîné le veut ; l'autre le veut aussi.
"Tirons au doigt mouillé."—"Parbleu non."—"Parbleu si."

—"Cède, ou bien tu verras."—"Mais tu verras toi-même."
De propos en propos, l'aîné, peu patient,   20
    Jette à la tête de son frère
Le perdreau disputé. Le cadet, en colère,
    D'un des siens riposte à l'instant.
    L'aîné recommence d'autant;
Et ce jeu qui leur plaît couvre autour d'eux la terre   25
    De pauvres perdreaux palpitants.
Le fermier, qui passait en revenant des champs,
    Voit ce spectacle sanguinaire,
    Accourt, et dit à ses enfants
"Comment donc! petits rois, vos discordes cruelles   30
Font que tant d'innocents expirent par vos coups!
De quel droit, s'il vous plaît, dans vos tristes querelles,
    Faut-il que l'on meure pour vous?"

NOTES

LES DEUX VOYAGEURS

THIS Fable is No. 4 of Book I. in the ordinary French editions of Florian. In the notes on the other fables it will be considered sufficient to give the reference (as above) on the right of the number in this edition.

LINE

1. **compère.** One who is Godfather to another man's child is called the man's 'compère,' as sharing with him the responsibility of a 'père' in the things of GOD. The child would call him 'parrain.' As parents choose, of course, persons they like and esteem to be Godfathers to their children, the word has grown to mean generally 'a good fellow'—"*Master Thomas.*"

2. **tous deux** = 'both of them,' or, as we say, 'the two of them.' Notice the masc. pl. of 'tout.'

   ville = 'town.' In classical Latin *villa* is a 'country house,' but it gradually took the place of *urbs*, which has disappeared in French.

4. **louis (d'or),** a gold coin now worth 20 francs (in Florian's time *24* francs), about 16s. in English money.

5. **d'un air content** = 'with a pleased look.'

6. **aubaine** signified originally the property of a stranger, which, by ancient law, came into the public treasury. Received unexpectedly, it was looked upon as a lucky gain ; hence the meaning 'a windfall.'

7. **froidement.** Notice the ending 'ment' added to the feminine form of the adjective to make the adverb. It is the Latin word *mente* (abl. of *mens*, the mind); *frigida mente* (= with cold mind) was changed to *froidement*. So *viva mente* (= with lively mind) became *vivement*, and others in the same way.

8. **Pour nous.** He repeats his friend's words, making them the subject of *est*. 'The phrase "for us" is not well said, "for me" is a different thing.'

moi. This is the accusative case after the preposition *pour*, but the word has come, like *toi* and *lui*, to be used very often for the subject of a sentence; *moi qui ris* = I who laugh.

9. **ne souffle plus** = 'makes no more to-do.'

10. **au bois voisin** = 'in the neighbouring wood.'

12. **lui,** the Latin *illi huic* = 'to this one,' was contracted to *illuic*, and then *illui :* losing its first syllable, it became *lui*, like *la* (*illam*), *leur* (*illorum*), etc.

13. **c'est autre chose** = 'that's quite another thing.'

14. **s'échappe,** formerly *escaper*, 'to get out of one's *cappa*' (Italian for *cape* or *cloak*); hence to *escape* or *flee away*. We have an exact analogy in the Greek ἐκδύω = 'strip off,' 'put off'; hence 'escape,' as in ἐκδῦμεν ὄλεθρον (*Il.* xvi. 99), 'escape from death.'

16. **la donne** = 'gives it' to the robbers, of course.

II. (i. 18)

LA TAUPE ET LES LAPINS

2. **En convenir,** 'to own any of them.'

4. **avouer,** a term of feudal right; 'avouer un seigneur' meant to *recognise as one's superior the feudal lord,* and 'vouer à lui,' *to swear obedience to him,* and show it in action; hence the general meaning—*avow, confess.*

   qu'ils en sont cause, 'people prefer to suffer real ills than allow that they are the cause of them'; rather an awkward sentence. 'En' is used instead of 'd'eux' when speaking of *things.*

9. **le soir,** 'one evening.'

12. **colin-maillard.** *Colin,* according to Littré, is the name of a man who is *caught,* generally. *Maillard* comes from *maillot* (*maille* from Lat. *macula*), and means 'swaddling band'; hence, 'Il était encore au maillot,' 'he was still in his cradle.'

14. **Rien n'est plus vrai pourtant,** 'nothing is more true, for all that.'

15. **en bandeau,** 'like a bandage.'

17. **Un instant en faisait l'affaire,** 'the thing was done in a moment.'

20. **faisaient merveilles.** A phrase used of doing anything unusually well; here it is 'performed wonders.'

23. **soudain;** this is the adverb 'suddenly.'

24. **pot au noir,** proverbial expression drawn from a game in which one ran risk of blacking one's hands; hence a 'snare.'

   hasard, in the twelfth century, meant the game of dice; later it came to mean the chances of the game. In Arabic *al-sár* means 'the game of dice.'

32. **n'y voyant pas,** 'not seeing anything there.' *Y*, in Old French *iv* and then *i*, is the Latin *ibi*.

34. **conscience,** 'a question of conscience.'

36. **Nous fassions,** etc., 'that we favour our poor sister a little'; here *faveur* is used of an indulgence which is not granted to everybody.

39. **de bon jeu,** 'in fair play,' 'fairly caught.'

44. **encor,** in poetry for *encore*, formerly *ancore*.

III. (i. 19)

LE ROSSIGNOL ET LE PRINCE

1. **gouverneur.** A tutor or governor, such as each of our young princes has had, with charge of the moral as well as the intellectual training.

4. **C'est le profit de la grandeur,** 'it is the privilege of greatness'; *the penalty* would have been perhaps nearer the truth.

7. **dans le moment,** 'at the instant,' 'that moment.'

8. **L'attraper** is derived from *trappe*, from the Latin word belonging to the Middle Ages, *trappa*. Its origin is German, like that of most words connected with the chase. High German *trapo*, a 'snare,' 'trap.'

13. **farouche,** not 'fierce,' though it often means this ; simply 'wild.'

15. **Mentor,** a wise counsellor and friend. *Mentor* was the guide and friend of Telemachus. See Fénelon's *Télémaque*.

18. **il faut l'aller trouver.** We should now rather say, 'il faut aller le trouver.'

IV. (i. 20)

L'AVEUGLE ET LE PARALYTIQUE

1. **Aidons-nous mutuellement,** 'let us help each other.' *Mutuellement* need not be further translated.

2. **en,** here in the sense of 'on that account,' 'all the more.' Cf. line 15 below.

3. **l'on,** the Latin *homo* became successively *hom*, *om* (by dropping the initial and unaspirated '*h*,' as in 'habere' = 'avoir'), and finally *on*.

5. **Confucius,** the lawgiver and founder of the religion of China, B.C. 550.

7. **trait,** properly a 'stroke,' 'shot' from a *drawn* bow ; here a happy 'incident.'

10. **perclus,** 'one who has lost the use of all his limbs'; 'a paralytic'; 'a cripple.'

LINE

12. 'But their cries were useless.' Cri is the noun derived from the verb *crier*. The Latin *quiritare*, 'to wail,' by contraction became *q'ritare*, then *criter*, lastly *crier*.

13. **paralytique**, from the Greek παραλυτικός.

15. **il en souffrait bien plus**, 'he only suffered the more.' A beautiful line, expressing admirably the wretchedness of suffering without sympathy.

20. **il arriva**, 'it happened.' The difference between the French and English idiomatic use of 'arrive' was capitally illustrated by one of John Leech's pictures in *Punch* some years ago. A polite Frenchman meets an old-fashioned Quaker in the gray coat with stand-up collar that is so rarely seen nowadays. He goes up to him, and, raising both hands, turns the collar down with the apology, '*Pardon, M'sieur, it has arrived to your collair to stick him up.*'

22. **Près du malade se trouva**, inversion used in poetic diction only ; alter the order of the words to *se trouva près du malade*.

23. **en fut émue**, 'was moved by them'; notice the gender of 'émue.'

25. Virgil puts the same true sentiment into the mouth of Queen Dido (*Æn*. i. 630): '*Non ignara mali miseris succurrere disco.*'

31. **A quoi nous servirait**, 'what good would it do us ?'

36. **mal assuré**, 'ill-assured,' 'uncertain.'

37. **vous voudrez**; notice the future tense. In English we say, '*wherever you wish*'; in French, 'wherever you will wish.'

38. **sans que jamais notre amitié décide**, 'without our friendship ever deciding'—we will never quarrel as to who does most.

39. **emploi**, *business, station, post ;* here used to express the part taken by an actor : 'which of us two fills the best rôle ?'

40. **vous y verrez pour moi**, 'you will see for me.' 'Y redundant, y voir,' *to be able to see.* Cf. the idiom : 'Je n'y vois goutte,' *I cannot see (understand) at all.*

V. (ii. 1)

LA MÈRE, L'ENFANT, ET LES SARIGUES

3. **bruyère.** *Brugaria** is the diminutive of a Breton word—'brûg' = 'heath.'

5. **renard.** The name *Renard*, by which the fox is known in English as well as French, is a *Proper name*. There is a celebrated epic poem of the Middle Ages (*Roman de Renard*), in which all the animals are known by Proper names which have been given them. The lion is *Noble*, the bear *Brun* (our Bruin), the cock *Chante-Clair* (our *Chanticleer*), the fox *Renart*. In the twelfth century *renart* began to be used instead of the original word *goulpil* and *vulpicula*, and soon *goupil* was retained only to

LINE

mean a *young fox*. The derivation of Renard is curious. The word is the same as Reginald or Reginhalt, from the German words *ragin = counsel*, and *hart = hard* or *quick*: so Renard meant 'one good in counsel,' 'cunning.'

The opossum is not really like the fox; it is a mammiferous animal belonging to the order *marsupial*, and, like the kangaroo, has a pouch in which it carries its young. *Sarigue*, pronounced *sareeg*, is a corruption of the Brazilian word *Çarigueya*.

14. **ce qu'ils vont devenir**, 'what will become of them.' Notice the difference of construction between *devenir* and *to become*.

17. **d'accourir, a** sort of infinitive of narration—'the little ones at once (begin to) run up.'

21. **blottis**, 'squatted.' 'Se blottir' is a term in falconry used of the bird when he squats on his perch to go to sleep. It has come to mean generally, 'to lie close.'

23-27. It gives pathetic interest to these lines to remember that Florian's mother died when he was quite young, and he always regretted his irreparable loss. One day, seeing a child weeping because his mother had whipped him, he exclaimed, 'How happy you are that you *can* be whipped by a *mother!*'

24. **La Péruvienne**, 'the Peruvian lady.'

VI. (ii. 2)

LE VIEUX ARBRE ET LE JARDINIER

6. **Le voilà qui prend sa cognée**, ' *There he is, taking his axe!*' 'Cognée' was in Old French written 'coignée,' from the Latin *cuneatam* = 'wedge-shaped.' The Latin *cuneum* gives 'coin' = *wedge*.

7. **coup.** The Latin word *colpus* is found in the *Lex Salica*, tit. 19, and is a contracted form of *colapus*, altered from Lat. *colaphus* = 'a blow with the fist.'

10. **La mort va me saisir.** Notice the use of 'aller ' to express the *immediate* future; lit. as in English 'is going to.'

11. **N'assassine pas un mourant**, 'do not murder a dying creature.' The word assassin is of historical origin. In Low Latin it is *hassessin*—the name of a celebrated sect of Palestine in the thirteenth century, who used to drink an intoxicating drug made from powdered hemp leaves and called *haschisch* until they were sufficiently excited to go out and murder any one who came in their way. So Haschischin came to mean simply *murderers*, and in the fifteenth century its altered form 'assassin' was in ordinary use to denote 'one who slays with a poniard,' or 'murderer.'

14. **gazouillant à la fois**, 'warbling together.'

17. **Lorsque**; 'lors,' formerly written 'l'ore,' is the Latin *illa hora*, 'at

that hour.' The two parts of the word are still separated sometimes, as 'lors *même* que.'

18. **ramage** is usually 'flowered work' ('ouvrage à ramage')—the re-
presentation of boughs in needlework ; here it is clearly 'our
sweet *singing in its branches*.'

19. **ennui** has so peculiarly a meaning of its own that it has been
half adopted into English ; 'downright weariness from having
nothing to do' is perhaps the best expression for it.

22. **en lui disant,** 'saying to him.' 'En' need not be translated. This
is a very common use of 'en,' *e.g.* 'parler en tremblant,' 'to
speak trembling,' etc. 'En' is the only prep. that takes the
present participle, all others require the infinitive.

26. **Un miel délicieux**; in construing omit 'un.'

27. **rayon** is usually a 'ray'—'rayons de lumière,' 'rays of light' ;
'rayons du soleil,' 'the sun's rays'; 'une étoile à cinq rayons,'
'a five-pointed star'; 'rayon de miel,' 'honeycomb.'

28. **Cela te touche-t-il?** 'There ! does that move you ?'

J'en pleure de tendresse, 'I weep with pity for it.' ·

32. **quelquefois**; 'quel' is the Latin *qualem ;* 'que' = Lat. *quod ;*
'fois,' Lat. *vicem.*

33. **C'en est assez pour moi,** 'that (that I have just said) is enough for
me.' The use of the relative 'en' is often a difficulty with young
students of French. Here it is used as complement of 'assez,'
where in English we do not require any word ; and often it takes
the place of 'son,' 'sa,' 'ses,' 'leur' after one of these possessives
has been employed in the first part of a sentence. For example,
we say, 'Le livre a son mérite,' 'The book has its worth '; but
if we added, 'every one appreciates its value,' we should say,
'tout le monde en apprécie la valeur,' not 'tout le monde
apprécie sa valeur.'

qu'ils chantent en repos, 'let them sing in peace.'

35. **de fleurs semer tout ce canton** would mean ordinarily, '*strew*
with flowers all this canton' or district; here it is clearly
'plant with flowers the whole district.' ·

38. **reconnaissance,** 'reward for past services'; the common meaning is 'gratitude.'

39. **Quand l'intérêt vous en répond,** 'when self-interest gives you
its word for it.'

VII. (iii. 16)

LE PAON, LES DEUX OISONS, ET LE PLONGEON

('Paon,' pronounced like *pan.*)

1. **faisait la roue,** 'was spreading his tail.' 'Roue' properly means
a 'wheel,' as in the phrase 'mettre des bâtons dans la roue' ('to

LINE

put a spoke in the wheel'); so 'fait la roue' is used of a street arab who 'makes a cart-wheel' on hands and feet.

2. **brillant**, 'sparkling like a beryl.' The beryl (Greek βήρυλλος) is an emerald of pure sea-green colour. The verb derived from it became 'bryllare,' and so 'briller' = 'to sparkle.'

3. **oisons**, derived from 'oie,' Lat. *aucam*, found in writings of the Middle Age ('accipiter qui aucam mordet').

nasillard is used as an adj. or subs. ; 'parler d'un ton nasillard,' 'speak in a snuffling tone'; 'c'est un nasillard,' 'he's a snuffler.'

6. **Comme ses pieds sont plats**, 'how flat his feet are'; notice this idiomatic use of 'comme,' always separated from the adjective which it qualifies. 'Comme vous êtes stupide,' 'how stupid you are.'

8. **fait fuir jusqu'à la chouette** ; 'jusqu'à,' here *even;* say—'scares even the owl away.'

9. **riait . . . du mal qu'il avait dit**, 'laughed at the spiteful thing he had said.'

10. **plongeon**, a 'sea-mew,' 'diver'; 'faire le plongeon' = 'to duck the head.'

11. **d'une lieue**, 'a mile off.'

12. **j'en conviens**, 'I admit it,' 'I agree to it.'

VIII. (ii. 8)

L'ENFANT ET LE MIROIR

1. **village**, derived from *villa*, 'a country house'; see note to i. 2. The French have a proverb which conveys the same idea as the first part of this fable, 'il est bien de son village,' 'he does not know what is going on in the world.'

2. **chez**, an elliptical form ; in Old French, 'à ches,' or 'en chiés' = 'à la maison.'

5. **travers**, 'whim,' 'caprice.' They say of a woman who is very eccentric, 'elle a de grands travers.'

8. **Lui fait une grimace**, 'makes a face at it.'

11. **de même**, 'in the same way.'

12. **marmot**, 'our little brat.' The orig. sense of *monkey* is obsolete. We have the form 'marmosette' from Fr. 'marmouset.'

s'en vient . . . battre, 'goes so far as to strike.'

14. **Il se fait mal aux mains**, 'he hurts his own hands.' 'Mal' is the common word for 'ache' or 'pain'; 'mal à la tête,' 'head-ache'; 'mal de mer,' 'sea-sickness.'

15. **au désespoir**, 'in despair.' 'J'en suis au désespoir,' 'I am very troubled about it.'

16. **Le voilà**, 'there he is.'

LINE

19. **pleurs,** 'flood of tears'; a plural word. 'Larme' is the ordinary word for 'a tear.'

21. **méchant,** 'naughty,' said playfully. 'Méchant' is generally put before the noun it qualifies ; placed after its noun it means 'ill-natured'; 'un méchant homme,' 'a bad man'; 'un homme méchant,' 'an ill-natured man.'

22. **Oui,** the Latin *hoc illud.* In Old French it was written as a word of two syllables—'oïl.'

26. Do not translate the article **le** in this line ; 'le bien,' 'good.'

IX. (ii. 11)

LE GRILLON

4. **Voltigeant,** 'fluttering about.' It is used also of gymnastic exercise on the wooden horse ; hence our word 'vault.'

6. **L'azur,** 'blue'; do not translate the article.

7. **de fleurs en fleurs,** 'from flower to flower.'

9. **que son sort et le mien sont différents** ; cf. note to 'comme,' vii. l. 6.

10. **Dame nature** ; we have the exact phrase, 'Dame Nature.'

13. **Nul ne prend.** Notice that 'nul' (like 'rien,' 'personne,' etc.) always requires the negative adverb 'ne' before its verb ; 'je n'en ai nulle connaissance,' 'I have no knowledge of it.'

 ici-bas, 'here below,' that is, 'in this world'; a similar use is 'ici-près,' 'hard by.'

14. **Autant vaudrait n'exister pas,** 'as well not exist at all !'

17. **courants.** The rule is, that the present participle does not agree with its noun unless it is used as an adjective. It is clearly not an adjective here, but the *s* is added to make it rhyme with 'enfants.'

18. **dont ils ont tous** (*s* sounded) **envie,** 'for which they all are eager.' Distinguish this 'envie,' a feminine noun, from the adverbial expression, 'à l'envi,' 'with emulation.'

24. **Il ne fallait pas tant d'efforts,** 'it did not need so many efforts.'

25. **déchirer,** from the Old High German *skerran,* 'to tear.'

26. **je ne suis plus fâché,** 'I am no longer distressed.'

27. **Il en coûte,** the 'en' cannot be construed ; simply, 'it costs too much,' etc.

X. (ii. 16)

LE DANSEUR DE CORDE ET LE BALANCIER

1. **Sur la corde tendue,** 'on the tight-rope.'

3. **tours de force,** 'feats of strength.' Another meaning of 'tour

LINE

de force' is 'a great crowning effort' by which one accomplishes some object.

4. **Faisaient venir maint spectateur**, 'brought many a spectator.' Notice the difference between the French and English idioms ; 'maint' does not require 'un' to be used with it, it is an indefinite adjective, and agrees with its noun ; 'mainte fois,' 'many a time.'

5. **qui s'avance**, 'advancing.'

6. **l'air libre**, 'with free motion.'

11. **en volant**, 'as they fly.'

eaux. 'Eau' is the Latin *aquam*. The *q* was first changed to *v* (as in 'sequere' = 'suivre'), and the word gradually changed to 'aqva,' 'ava,' 'eave,' 'eau.' In the sixteenth century it ceased to be a word of two syllables, and was pronounced, as now, *ô*.

12. **sans qu'on le voie** ('voie,' subj. after 'sans que'), 'without their seeing it,' *i.e.* 'without their seeing that his foot touched the rope.'

15. **A quoi bon**, 'What's the good of?' 'Why?'

16. **me fatigue et m'embarrasse.** Notice the repetition of the pronoun 'me,' which is not needed in English.

19. **Aussitôt fait que dit**, 'no sooner said than done.'

20. **Notre étourdi chancelle**, 'our thoughtless friend becomes unsteady.' 'Étourdie,' in the feminine, corresponds to our *madcap*.

21. **Il se casse le nez.** Notice the idiomatic use of the refl. pron. 'se,' and the art. 'le' for the possess. pron. 'son.'

22. **gens**, 'people.' 'Gent' in the singular is feminine gender, and in the plural masculine ; but a plural adjective used with it is put in the feminine if it *comes before* 'gens.'

23. **tôt ou tard**, 'sooner or later.' Used with a compound tense of the verb, 'tôt ou tard' (like many other adverbs) never comes between the auxiliary verb and the participle ; we say, 'il aura fini tôt ou tard,' but NEVER 'il aura tôt ou tard fini'; though we say quite rightly, 'il aura bientôt fini.'

24. **la vertu**, etc. Notice the use of the definite article before abstract nouns.

26. **C'est le balancier qui vous gêne**, 'it is the balancing-pole which is in your way.' In Corneille's time the word 'gêner' had its original meaning of *torture* (from 'gehenna,' 'the place of torment') ; since then it has been watered down to mean 'disquiet,' 'annoy,' 'embarrass.'

XI. (iv. 6)

LA VIPÈRE ET LA SANGSUE

2. **Que notre sort**, etc. ; see ix. 9.

8. **Cependant** = 'pendant cela,' 'that being in suspense'; 'and yet.'

piqûre, from the root 'pic'; whence the German *picken* and our own 'pick.'

9. **étang**; notice the change of initial *s* followed by *t, p, c* into *é*— *statum* = 'état'; *studium* = 'étude'; *stellam* = 'étoile,' etc. etc. This is accounted for by the difficulty which people had in pronouncing initial *s* followed by a consonant without a vowel in front of it. To help themselves they put an *i* before the *s* and said 'ispatium,' 'istare,' 'istabilem'; and these forms are found in the inscriptions of the fourth century. Soon the *i* changed to *e;* they said 'esprit,' 'espace,' 'estable'; a further change was made, and from the sixteenth century onwards we read 'étable,' 'école' (*scholam*), 'écriture' (*scripturam*), etc. etc. ; many words, however, retained the *s; e.g.* 'esprit,' 'espace,' 'escient,' 'espérer,' etc.

10. **Oh ! que nenni**, 'Oh! not so at all.' The old form 'nenil,' found in the twelfth century, points to the derivation *non illud.*

15. **Je suis remède.** Notice that the French do not use the indefinite article *here* as we do—' I am a remedy, you a poison.'

XII. (iv. 10)

L'Avare et son Fils

2. **Se bien traiter** ordinarily means to 'live well,' to 'keep a good table'; probably it would be best-translated here 'to give himself a treat.'

7. **Ferma les doubles tours de sa double serrure,** 'turned the double bolts of his double lock'; 'fermer à double tour' = 'to double-lock.' This is an awkward line, and not easy to translate, though the meaning is clear enough.

11. **quelqu'une de pourrie,** 'a rotten one.'

13. **faisant fort maigre chère,** 'living very poorly'; 'faire bonne chère à quelqu'un' is 'to feast any one.'

14. **à la fin,** 'at last.

15. **clefs,** pronounced 'clay.'

17. **dégât.** There is a German word *wastjan* (English 'waste'), which Littré says has helped to change the *v* of *vastare* into *g*.

20. **De douleur, d'effroi palpitant,** 'panting with grief and fright.'

22. 'Or I will have you all hung !'

24. **personne** is a noun and is feminine gender, like the Latin *personam*, when it has the article or an adjective agreeing with it, as in 'cette personne est très bonne'; but when used as an indefinite pronoun, as in 'personne n'est venu' ('nobody came'), it is masculine.

XIII. (iv. 17)

LE CHAT ET LES RATS

LINE

1. **Angora,** a town in Asia Minor (Ἄγκυρα), so called from the anchors of vessels which Ptolemy, King of Egypt, had sent to the help of the people of Galatia, and which were captured by Mithridates. It is celebrated for having a special breed of cats and of goats, with long silky hair (Persian cat).

5. **ne se gênaient pas,** 'took their ease,' did not disquiet themselves with the thought of their enemy the cat.

7. **festin.** Littré says it is derived from the Latin *festivum.* Brachet gives Italian *festino.*

10. **ne bougeait.** Notice the omission of 'pas,' as in the case of 'pouvoir,' 'savoir,' 'oser,' 'cesser.'

13. **fort,** 'very highly.' 'J'ai cela fort à cœur,' 'I have that very much at heart.'

15. **tribunal,** properly 'seat of a judge'; but here used instead of 'tribune.' The tribune in the Chamber of Deputies is the rostra from which every speaker addresses the house. The members do not speak each rising in his place as in our House of Commons.

17. **De ce grain désormais nous devons être las,** lit. 'we must from this day forward be tired of this grain.' 'Désormais' is made up of 'dès,' Lat. *de-ex,* 'ore,' Lat. *hora,* and 'mais,' Lat. *magis,* 'from the present hour to a later.'

19. **On les dit excellents,** 'people say they (*i.e.* cats) are excellent.'

    nous en ferons bombance, 'we will feast on them.'

23. **comme on croit,** 'as one can well believe.'

24. **Couche bientôt sur la poussière,** 'soon lays in the dust.'

25. **tribun**; the Tribune was (1) a magistrate chosen by the Romans to protect the rights of the people; or (2) as here, an officer in charge of a sixth part of a legion.

26. **Il ne s'échappa que deux rats;** 'il' is used impersonally—'there.'

30. **gagner.** From the German *Weida* = 'pasture,' and the verb *weid-anjan,* the French got the words 'gagnage' and 'gagner' (formerly written 'gaaigner') with the same meaning; from this there came a general idea of profit derived from rural labour; and thence we get the meaning of profit from labour of any kind—*gain.*

XIV. (iv. 18)

LE MIROIR DE LA VÉRITÉ

1. **siècle d'or,** the 'golden age' of purity, abundance, and peace.

3. **Coulaient des jours,** 'spent quietly their days.'

E

12. **de dépit,** 'in vexation.'

14. **au hasard,** 'at random.' Notice that the *h* is aspirated.

16. **on en connut le prix,** 'men recognised its value'; for 'en . . . le,' cf. note to vi. 33.

21. **le sage le premier.** Notice the adverbial use of 'le premier' (cf. Lat. 'qui *primus* ab oris').

XV. (ii. 6)

Le Bouvreuil et le Corbeau

4. **ménage** is properly the 'expenses of a house'; *mansionaticum* occurs with the same meaning in the Carlovingian texts, and was changed to 'maisnage,' 'mesnage,' and finally 'ménage.'

6. **fromage.** Papias quotes *formaticum* as the popular word for *caseum ;* and Ducange quotes a text of the ninth century, 'ova manducant et formaticum id est caseum.' Cheese has always had its peculiar *form,* hence the name.

8. **Afin qu'il voulût . . . se taire,** 'that he might consent (be good enough) to be quiet.'

10. **pour l'ordinaire,** 'generally.'

13. **de son chant l'harmonie ;** inversion allowed in poetic diction only.

16. **ils n'y pensaient pas,** 'they did not think of it,' *i.e.* of looking to see if his trough was filled.

18. **il chantait si bien.** When this fable was written, Florian was no doubt grieving over the death of Malfilâtre, a poet, who had died in great distress, like our own Chatterton and many another.

19. **Certes.** The complete phrase is 'à certes' (*voies* or *choses* understood) from the Latin *a certis* (*rebus*). *Certus* by metathesis for *cretus.*

20. **Le corbeau crie encore,** 'the raven keeps on screaming' to the present day.

XVI (iii. 20).

Le Lion et le Léopard

3. **forêt.** Diez derives this word from the Latin *foris,* 'out of doors.'

4. **léopard,** from λέων and πάρδος. In poetry and oratory Léopard was the French name for England ; Voltaire describes the famous warrior, Du Guesclin, as going forth 'briser les léopards.'

5. **attaquer** is the Flemish and Picard pronunciation of 'attacher' ('à' and 'tacher').

LINE
7. **cour**, used here in its primitive sense, 'a rural domain,' and formerly written 'court' or 'curt.' The Latin from which it is drawn is *cortem* or *curtem*, au abbreviated form of *cohortem;* it is in Greek χόρτος, from the same root as *hortus*, and the German *Garten*, 'garden.'

8. **Voici comment s'y prit notre monarque habile**, 'this is the method our crafty monarch took.' 'S'y prendre' = 'to go about'. any business, to set to work at anything. 'Se prendre' = 'to lay hold of.'

10. **ambassadeur**, from *ambactus*, used by Cæsar, *B. G.* vi. 15 ; the Old High German *Ambaht* (Anglo-Saxon *aembcht*) = 'servant' is preferred by Diez.

13. **douceur**, 'gentleness.' The word itself has passed into our language, and denotes that which helps to sweeten toil, 'a *gratuity*,' 'a *tip*.'

18. **le lendemain**. There is here an unconscious doubling of the article 'le.' The word 'lendemain,' formerly written 'l'ende-main,' is the abbreviation of 'le jour en demain' ('demain,' Lat. *de mane*). In the fourteenth century there arose a curious mistake—the mistake, no doubt, of ignorance—and the article was doubled, so that we find 'le l'endemain,' which soon changed to the present form. There is a similar mistake in our English, 'the alligator,' alligator being the Spanish *al lagarto* = '*the* lizard.'

19. **frontières**, *frontiers, borders*. The word 'frontière' formerly meant simply *front*, and 'faire frontière' was to set troops in array for fighting or for defence. As this most frequently was done on the *borders* of the territory to be attacked or defended, 'frontière' came to mean *border*.

20. **à qui mieux mieux**, an adverbial expression meaning 'in emula-tion one of another,' very like 'à l'envi.'

22. **Partageant le pays conquis**, 'dividing into shares the conquered country.' Notice that 'partageant,' used as the participle, does not alter, though 'les rois amis' (*the two king-friends*) is plural. 'Pays' is pronounced 'pay-yee.'

24. **Il s'éleva**, 'there arose.'

28. **on en vint aux coups**, 'they came to blows.' 'En venir *aux mains*' has the same meaning.

29. **trépas**, '*step beyond* the limits of life.'

XVII. (ii. 7)

LE SINGE QUI MONTRE LA LANTERNE MAGIQUE

1. **Messieurs les beaux esprits**, 'the wits,' or, used disparagingly, as it is here, 'the witlings.' We cannot translate 'Messieurs.' It is peculiarly a French idiom. When we say, 'Your brother,'

LINE

a Frenchman, except when on terms of intimacy, would say '*Monsieur* votre frère.'

2. **toujours admirable,** spoken ironically, 'always very fine indeed.'

3. **Mais que l'on n'entend point,** 'which, however, one does not understand in the least.' Notice the use of the conjunction 'mais' before the *relative* ('que') *occurring for the first time in a sentence.* It is a mistake often made in English, and must be carefully guarded against. The relative pronoun used *for the first time in a sentence ought* NEVER to have a conjunction before it. For instance, in the sentence : 'The town, seen for the first time, and which we neared at great speed'—the '*and*' is quite wrong, and ought not to be there. 'The flowers, so exquisite upon the mountain-top, but which lost all their brilliance in passing through the post, can only be put right by omitting the '*but*' and inserting '*however*' after the relative '*which.*'

7. **Attiraient ;** 'tirer' is, according to Littré, from the Old High German *zeran,* Gothic *tairan,* our English 'tear.'

9. **Dansait et voltigeait au mieux,** 'was one of the best dancers and vaulters in the world.'

10. **le saut périlleux,** 'the somersault.'

13. **tout du long,** 'all the time'; not, as the phrase often means, 'at full length.'

14. **à la prussienne,** 'in Prussian style'; *i.e.* smartly, briskly, correctly.

16. **un jour de fête,** 'a holiday'; 'a saint's day,' 'one's birthday.'

18. **Veut faire un coup de sa tête,** 'wishes to show how clever he is.' From the frequency with which people try to do this and fail, the phrase is often used to mean 'make a great blunder.'

21. **dindons.** The turkey, 'this noble bird,' as Prescott calls him, was brought into Europe from the West Indies, where he had been seen by Oviedo, who is the first naturalist to describe him. When the Spaniards conquered Mexico, they found the turkey both tame and wild. They called him *gallopavo,* because he spreads his tail like the peacock (*pavo*). When first imported the French called him 'coq d'Inde' (*Indian fowl*) ; they soon dropped the 'coq' and called him 'dinde,' and 'dindon'; 'dinde' eventually becoming the feminine, and 'dindon' the masculine name. Prescott, in his *Conquest of Mexico* (i. 185), calls the wild turkey 'the pride of the American forest.'

22. **à la file,** 'in Indian file,' as we say ; 'one behind the other.'

23. **entrez, etc.** This is very like *our* showman's invitation, 'Walk up, walk up, ladies and gentlemen ; here you have,' etc. etc.

25. **gratis,** *s* sounded ; we have taken the word into our language, keeping the same meaning, *free* (*of free grace*). It has acquired a new meaning in the phrase 'advice gratis'; advice which, being given unasked, is thought little of. *Gratuitous,* derived from it, has an unpleasant sense. 'Gratuitous remarks'

LINE

are generally unpleasant remarks that there was no necessity to make.

37. **Est-il rien de pareil?** 'Is there anything to equal it?' 'est-il' used impersonally.

38. **soleil,** a diminutive of *solem* not found in the other Romance languages. Spanish and Portuguese *sol*, Italian *sole*.

46. **L'appartement,** from the Latin *partiri,* meaning literally 'that which is divided.'

50. **Ni moi non plus,** 'nor I either.'

51. **je vois,** etc., 'I see *something* quite well, but I do not know why I don't distinguish very clearly (what it is).' A good hit at some conceited people who will not allow that they do not see *what they think other people see.*

54. **le Cicéron moderne ;** the name is used, of course, in allusion to the eloquence of the great orator, 'our modern Cicero.' The Italian *cicérone* (final *e* pron. = *é*) now means a guide who explains to strangers the sights and curiosities of a place. It is pronounced in Italian fashion, *tchi-tchéroné.*

57. **d'éclairer sa lanterne,** 'to light up his lantern'; 'éclairer' means to put or show a light to any one or any thing ; 'éclairez Monsieur,' *light the gentleman.*

XVIII. (ii. 22)

LE LINOT

1. **Linot, linotte.** A little gray bird with sweet song, so called from its great liking for the grain 'lin' (*linum,* flax—*linseed*). Buffon the great naturalist tells of a linnet who could say, 'Pretty boy,' and was visited by thousands of people at his home in Kensington.

5. **Sa mère en était folle,** 'his mother doted on him,' 'was quite silly about him.'

6. **Que peuvent inventer,** etc. Notice the position of the relative pronoun in the objective case, *before the verb which governs it,* while the subject comes, *in position, after the verb.*

9. **Se croyait un phénix,** 'thought himself a wonderful bird,' with no other like him—'a paragon.' The Phœnix is a fabulous bird, said to live for 500 years (in Arabia), or, according to Richardson, for 1000 years. Then it makes for itself a nest of spices, sets the nest on fire, and dies singing a melodious song ; but out of its own ashes it rises to life again, to live another 500 years. Shakespeare has an allusion similar to this in our text—

'If she be furnish'd with a mind so rare,
She is alone the Arabian bird.'—*Cymbeline,* I. vi. 16.

prenait l'air suffisant, 'put on a self-conceited air.'

10. **Tranchait du petit important avec,** 'lorded it over . . .'

LINE

13. **Donnait à chacun son paquet,** 'gave to each a sharp answer that silenced him,' or, as we say, 'shut up everybody.'

14. **se faisait haïr,** 'made himself hated.' Notice this use of the infinitive active with the verb 'se faire.' 'Haïr' is the Anglo-Saxon *hatian,* English 'hate,' and in the eleventh century was written *hadir.*

21. **bon mot,** 'witticism.'

22. **en gémissait,** 'groaned over it,' 'bemoaned it.'

25. **Je vous réponds,** 'I warrant you,' 'I'll be bound.'

26. **Vous jugez des alarmes,** 'you can conceive the fears,' 'the fright.'

27. **du danger,** 'at the danger.'

28. **brûlait.** The Latin *perustulare** (from *perustus*) became 'brustulare,' 'brusler,' 'brûler.'

32. **pivert,** the *picus viridis* is a lovely green bird, found in England and most European countries, which runs up trees, tapping as it goes to frighten out the insects; in descending it comes backwards. The 'laugh' (as it is called) of the green wood-pecker is a harsh 'Glu Glu Glu Gluck,' which is quite startling when heard unexpectedly. It has a hard, wedge-shaped bill with which it bores into holes or rotten parts of boughs, and with its long tongue catches the insects and their eggs. 'The tongue is a very wonderful organ; it has the appearance of a silver ribbon, or rather, from its transparency, a stream of molten glass; and the rapidity with which it is protruded and drawn in is so great that the eye is dazzled in following its motion; it is flexible in the highest degree.' There are other species besides the green woodpecker, viz. the black, the great, and the lesser spotted, etc.

33. **fausset.** J. J. Rousseau derived this word from 'faux' ('fauces,' *the throat*), and proposed to write it 'faucet'; but the corresponding Italian word *falsetto* proves it to come from *falsum.*

34. **prit mal cette plaisanterie,** 'took offence at this joke.'

37. **Le dégoûte à jamais du métier** . . . **railleur,** lit. '*disgusts* him for ever with the rôle of jester.'

38. **Il lui restait,** 'there still remained for him.'

40. **fauvette,** diminutive of the German *falb.* Littré says the Latin *fulvus* has the same root, as also *fulgeo* and φλέγω. This bird is the Warbler, or the 'Black-cap,' the sweetest singer among the linnets.

XIX. (iii. 1)

LES SINGES ET LE LÉOPARD

1. **la main chaude,** a game in which one of the players, stooping or bending over, lays one of his hands, open, upon his back; the

LINE

other players come up and strike him on it until he guesses who has struck him. I believe it is sometimes called 'Hot-cockles.'

2. **guenon,** a long-tailed female monkey. It is thought by some to be derived from the Old High German *Quena,* 'a woman.'

mauricaud, *brown-skinned,* 'Moorish.' Littré spells it 'mori-caud,' and derives it from 'more,' Lat. *maurus,* through *morisque,* the name of the Moors of Spain after the fall of their empire.

4. **courbant son échine,** 'bending his back.'

8. **gambades,** 'romping.' Littré gives the derivation 'gambe,' an old form of 'jambe,' *the leg.*

12. **Tout tremble à son aspect,** 'every one trembles at sight of him.'

13. **je n'en veux à personne,** 'I bear no ill-will to any one.' 'En vouloir à' means '*to have* a spite or grudge against' any one.

15. **comme particulier,** 'as a private gentleman.'

20. **c'est ma fantaisie,** 'it's a whim of mine.'

25. **crurent à ce discours,** 'had faith in this speech.' The verb 'croire,' when used affirmatively, takes the indicative mood after it—'Je crois qu'elle est belle'; used *negatively,* or *in asking a question,* it may take the subjunctive. If the action has reference to the subject of the sentence, use the infinitive only—'Je crois entendre (parler),' 'I think I hear (some one speaking).'

27. **joviale,** through the Italian *giovale,* from the Latin *jovialem,* an adjective from Jovis, genitive singular of Jupiter.

31. **devina,** 'had no difficulty in guessing.'

32. **sans le dire,** 'without saying so.'

37. **avec les grands,** 'with great folks.'

XX. (iii. 12)

LES ENFANTS ET LES PERDREAUX

1. **fermier.** The word 'ferme' properly means *an agreement for rent,* and in particular the rent of rural territory. From that the meaning has been extended to the land thus rented—*the farm,* and the person who rents it is *the farmer,* 'fermier.' The derivation from Lat. *firmus* gives the old idea (now almost a thing of the past) of *stability, security,* in the letting of land.

espiègles, 'frolicsome,' 'tricky.' Littré gives the derivation, the German *Eulen* ('screech-owl'), and *Spiegel* ('mirror,' Lat. *specu-lum*). Ménage says that a certain Saxon named Till Ulespiegle, who lived about 1480, was very celebrated for his ingenious tricks. His biography was written in German, and afterwards translated into French under the title, '*Histoire joyeuse et récréa-tive de Till Ulespiegle lequel par aucunes fallaces ne se laissa sur-*

prendre ne tromper.' The word 'espiègle' thus came to be used of any one *full of tricks,* like Ulespiegle.

3. **enclos,** 'paddock.'

6. **joie,** the Latin neuter plurals (*-a* or *-ia*) were often curiously mis-taken for feminines singular, and in old texts we find such words as *pecoras,* a plural of *pecora* (which is itself the pl. of *pecus*), and many others. The change of the *g* of 'gaudia' into the *j* of 'joie' is found in other words, such as 'jumeau' (*gemellum*), 'jaune' (*galbinum*), 'joue' (*gautam**), etc.

    bambins, 'bantlings,' *brats.*

8. **couper les chemins,** 'to stop the paths'—*cut off* the ways of escape.

9. **n'ont pas assez de leurs mains,** 'have not hands enough of their own.'

11. **traînant l'aile,** 'hanging its wing.'

18. **Tirons au doigt mouillé,** 'let us draw lots'; done by one wetting a finger and the other guessing *which* finger.

    Parbleu ! an exclamation, a sort of oath, altered from 'par Dieù'! 'Parbleu non'! 'certainly not'!

20. **peu patient,** 'out of patience'; or it might well be translated here by the adverb 'impatiently.'

23. **D'un des siens riposte à l'instant,** 'instantly replies with one of his own.'

26. **pauvres perdreaux palpitants;** notice the alliteration, '*p*oor *p*alpitating *p*artridges.'

30. **petits rois,** 'petty kings': a term of reproach.

EXERCISES

I

1. My friend will go on foot to the town.
2. I found a purse in the wood.
3. Do not leave the road.
4. I was trembling without cause.
5. As for thee—thou art lost.
6. He will not escape from the robbers.
7. With a pleased look he pocketed two louis.
8. This is a great (*grand*) misfortune for us.
9. You will be lost if (*si*) you go through the wood.
10. He never (*ne—jamais*) thinks of himself alone.

II

1. He does not know the man (whom) you see here.
2. We remember having been very much astonished.
3. I was amusing myself, one evening, tying a ribbon.
4. Did you ever see rabbits playing at blind-man's-buff ?
5. We were all dancing and leaping around.
6. If a band is tied round my eyes I shall not be able to see.
7. You will all be there till to-morrow.
8. Moles live (*vivre*) under the ground and are blind.
9. Not seeing you, I shall go to the meadow.
10. The poor rabbit catches only the air with his paw.
11. I cannot tie a knot. Can you ?
12. Pardon me, my dear ; you can, and so can I.
13. It was necessary to say that.
14. He answered coldly and hastily.

III

1. The prince will take a walk with his friend.
2. The nightingale is singing in the grove.

3. I see it under the foliage.
4. Do you wish to catch the poor bird ?
5. His Highness has two palaces and a garden.
6. Can you hide your greatness ?
7. I said to him, " I will instruct her if she wishes it."
8. They will go and find their tutor.
9. Her Highness will stay in the palace.
10. We will all dance round if you will put yourself in the middle.
11. Those birds are wild, and would not sing in a cage.
12. He will soon go home, but not in anger.

IV

1. In this town everything is useful.
2. The people of China help each other.
3. The poor blind man has not even a dog.
4. I hear the cry of a wretched man in the street.
5. You find yourself in a public place.
6. What is the use of that teaching ?
7. My brother could not follow me.
8. It happened that I was without a friend.
9. I will be your guide, and you shall carry me.
10. They cannot take a single step without seeing it.
11. Their troubles will be less dreadful if they love one another.
12. I will help you, in your turn.
13. We were asking my brother to conduct us.
14. Our misfortunes are not such as you have known.
15. Everything they say is true.
16. My legs are young : let us walk.

V

1. The child was seated on his mother's knee.
2. The opossum has a deep pouch.
3. If you make a noise the little ones will run up.
4. I shall flee away with my riches.
5. You do not remember my voice.
6. We shall all disappear into the wood.
7. The mother replied, " My boy, they were like foxes."
8. The blind man answered in a plaintive voice.
9. Clap your hands, and I will come.

10. Never put yourself in danger.
11. I have seen that animal only in a cage.
12. They wished (*comp. tense*) to take a walk yesterday.
13. A noise will frighten the thief.
14. She has lost all her tenderness.
15. I see him every day, and will give it him.

VI

1. We have some old pear-trees in our garden.
2. They have grown old, and are barren.
3. The gardener does not remember all the fruit they used to bear.
4. He wishes to cut them down, and seizes his axe.
5. He says he wants wood for the house.
6. I will come and sit by myself under their shade.
7. The nightingales will sing, and will charm me.
8. A swarm of bees came out of the trunk.
9. Bees often make their honeycomb in old trees.
10. The miserly old gardener likes this delicious honey.
11. He sells it and makes a profit by it.
12. Let the birds sing and the bees live in peace.
13. He will not cut down the old pear-tree.
14. But this is not gratitude, it is self-interest.
15. How ungrateful men are !
16. Help me to plant the garden with flowers.

VII

1. I admire the peacock's brilliant plumage.
2. Other birds cannot spread their tails as he does.
3. His feet are flat and ugly.
4. How disagreeable his cry is !
5. We see a gosling and a diver in the marsh.
6. They are laughing at the unkind things they have said.
7. They do not notice his beautiful tail.
8. And they do not remember their own ugly feet.
9. I can see him a mile off.
10. Let us amuse ourselves with the birds.
11. We shall never find that rabbit.
12. The poor gardener is losing (*perdre*) all his flowers.
13. You are as blind as a mole.

VIII

1. The child will return to his parents' home.
2. He will be surprised to see the large mirror there.
3. He will see his own image in it.
4. At first he will be very pleased.
5. But when he makes an ugly face in the glass,
6. And does not know that the mirror will make it back,
7. He will be very angry and will cry.
8. His mother will come unexpectedly and console him.
9. She will wipe away his tears and tell him the cause of his anger.
10. She will make him smile and the image will smile too.
11. Then he will see that he caused his own annoyance.
12. And he will be no longer angry.
13. There you are, my little bird, singing in the boughs.
14. I will hold out my hand to you and you will come.
15. Never return evil for good.

IX

1. I cannot see the crickets hidden in the grass.
2. The butterfly is fluttering about in the garden.
3. Look at its brilliant colours !
4. Gold and purple sparkle on its wings.
5. How happy the butterfly is !
6. They will do nothing for you but everything for him.
7. As I speak children arrive in the meadow.
8. They run after the insect with hats and caps.
9. If they catch it they will tear its wings.
10. One holds its body, another seizes its head.
11. I am very sorry that they have caught it at all.
12. It will never again fly from flower to flower.
13. The cricket lives happy in his quiet retreat.
14. The birds are hidden in the foliage.
15. I was laughing at the spiteful remark you made.
16. How different are your lot and mine.

X

1. The young acrobat will dance on the tight-rope.
2. With a balancing-pole he will be safe enough.
3. Many people come to see him.

4. He is light and brave and is quite happy on the rope.
5. He runs up and down with freedom (a free air),
6. Like a bird skimming the water.
7. One day he throws away his pole.
8. He says it is heavy and he can dance without it.
9. But he stumbles, and stretching out his hands,
0. Falls off the rope and breaks his nose.
11. Don't laugh ! You too need a balancing-pole,
12. Not to help you dance on a rope, but to live well.
13. Our passions cause us much pain ;
14. Virtue and reason are a rein upon them.
15. They dance with much grace.
16. We are very proud of our work.

XI

1. I will tell you what the Leech said one day.
2. The Viper was complaining
3. That their lots were very different. `
4. " People will look for you," she said, "and not fear you,
5. " But they kill me if they can catch me ;
6. " And yet we make the same wound."
7. The Leech answered from the marsh where she lived,
8. " No, no ! It is not the same wound !
9. " It is a little pricking that we both make,
10. " But mine cures people, yours kills them ;
11. " There is a great difference between a remedy and a
    poison."
12. What is the difference between satire and criticism ?
13. They often do good, both of them.
14. Satire is not altogether like a viper.

XII

1. A miser went one day to market
2. And bought himself some fine apples.
3. He carried them home and arranged them in his store-
    room,
4. And used to go and look at them almost every day,
5. But would not eat any until they began to go rotten,
6. And when he did eat one he sighed over it.
7. But he had a son, a young schoolboy, who liked apples ;

8. And one day, with a school-friend, he found the miser's treasure.
9. I do not know how he got the key ; but he did ;
10. And how many apples they ate, you may guess.
11. When they had just finished them, as it seems,
12. The old father came and caught them.
13. How angry he was ! How he shouted at them !
14. "Wretches ! where are my beautiful apples ?
15. "You shall both be hung ! You've eaten them all !"
16. His son replied, "Don't be put out, father !
17. "You only eat the bad (rotten) apples ;
18. "We haven't touched those ; we have eaten the good ones, and left you yours."

XIII

1. Don't feed your cat too well, or she will never catch the rats.
2. A kind mistress once fed her Angora
3. On dainty food, till he grew so easy-tempered
4. That he would not trouble himself about the rats,
5. And one day they held a meeting, without any fear.
6. Mr. Tom was sleeping after a good dinner;
7. And let them run about as they liked.
8. A young rat, climbing upon a bushel,
9. Told his friends how tired he was of corn,
10. As they all ought to be, and he was going for the future to eat cats.
11. "They're very good eating," he said, "let us begin."
12. No sooner said than done. They began.
13. Mr. Angora, suddenly awoke by their attack upon him;
14. Got up, and quickly killed them all,
15. Except two, who got (escaped) to their holes,
16. And never tried again to make war on the cats.
17. People ought to be contented.
18. We often lose what we might keep when we try to get too much.

XIV

1. The Age when men were good and pure and innocent
2. Was called the Golden Age.
3. Then Truth went about with her mirror,
4. Into which every one looked, and saw himself.

.5. Without blushing or being ashamed.
6. But when people became bad and untrue,
7. Truth fled to the skies, and her mirror, as it fell to the ground, was broken.
8. Men have found out the value of Truth since then,
9. And have looked for it everywhere ;
10. But the wisest men have only found fragments.
11. There is often much truth in satire ;
12. And criticism ought always to be just.

XV

1. People who perpetually ask for everything they see fatigue their friends, but often get what they wish ; while those who are modest and quiet are sometimes forgotten altogether.

2. The bullfinch in our fable sang only to give pleasure to every one, and they let him die of hunger ; but fed the raven, who was always asking for something to eat.

3. When he was dead they were all sorry. "What a pity," they said ; "he used to sing so sweetly." Many a sweet singer among men has died of hunger.

XVI

1. In a large plain there lived a lion, who, though he had a goodly heritage of his own, was not content, but wanted that of his neighbour the leopard.

2. The leopard received his ambassador, the monkey, and made an alliance with the lion to kill all the bears and panthers around them.

3. But when the two kings came to share the conquered territory, they quarrelled ; and the leopard found, when too late, that he had killed his friends, who had been a good barrier to him against his enemy the lion.

XVII

1. If we wish people to understand us, we must write clearly ; a pompous style in prose or verse is never good.

2. This fable tells how a monkey, very clever at tricks, who could dance, and walk on the tight-rope, and turn somersaults, one day tried to show his master's magic-lantern.

3. He put in the painted slides, and told his audience what they were,—the sun, the moon, the animals,—but nobody could see anything, for he had not lighted up the lantern.

4. So unless you light your lantern—*i.e.* are clear in style,—people will not see what you mean, though you may think you are writing very well.

XVIII

1. Many people make themselves hated by being conceited and rude in giving sharp answers and quizzing others.

2. The young linnet in our fable was taught a great lesson by the magpie and other birds in the wood, who misunderstood his "chaffing," and thought him impudent.

3. He learnt by adversity to be modest and polite, and so became as charming as he had been odious.

4. Young men, going out into the great world, are wise if they learn the same lesson ; but they are wiser if they have not needed to learn it.

XIX

1. There is a curious game, which is played thus:—One of the party, bending over so as to hide his eyes, places one hand, open, upon his back, and is struck by the others, until he guesses who has hit him.

2. Some monkeys were playing one day, and the young Prince Leopard, hearing their merry gambols, came and joined them. At first they were afraid, but he was so *débonnaire* they soon gained confidence, and began again to play.

3. It was all very pleasant till he struck the hand, and drew blood each time. Then they escaped one by one, without saying a word about it, and left the prince to play alone.

XX

Spoiled children are always a trouble to the parents who spoil them, and to the parents' friends who try to be kind to them. Our fable tells of two boys who had never been taught to be kind and gentle towards others, and who, in their wicked quarrel, killed thirteen poor little partridges that they had caught when looking for birds' nests in the paddock. Their father, the farmer, called them "Petty Kings," as though they had power of life and death ; but if he had taught them, when they were younger, to be polite and gentle and considerate for their friends and each other, he would not have had to blame them for their cruelty to the young partridges.

DIALOGUES

I

1. I am going away.	*Je m'en vais.*
2. Read me that fable.	*Lisez-moi cette fable.*
3. Spell that word.	*Épelez ce mot-là.*
4. Do you think there are robbers here ?	*Croyez-vous qu'il y ait des voleurs ici ?*
5. Yes, I fancy so.	*Oui, je le crois.*
6. It is nearly two o'clock.	*Il est près de deux heures.*
7. Where is your godfather ?	*Où est monsieur votre parrain ?*
8. How pleased I am !	*Que je suis content !*
9. What a misfortune !	*Quel malheur !*
10. All is lost.	*Tout est perdu.*

II

1. Let us go into the garden.	*Entrons dans le jardin.*
2. Have you any carrots or cabbages ?	*Avez-vous des carottes ou des choux ?*
3. Yes, if the rabbits have not eaten them.	*Oui, si les lapins ne les ont pas mangés.*
4. What do I see under the tree ?	*Qu'est-ce que je vois sous l'arbre ?*
5. I do believe it's a mole !	*Je crois vraiment que c'est une taupe !*
6. Poor beast, it cannot see.	*Pauvre bête, elle n'y voit pas.*
7. The weather is very cold.	*Il fait très froid.*
8. The ground is quite frozen.	*La terre est toute gelée.*
9. Will it be able to burrow ?	*Pourra-t-elle faire un trou ?*
10. I do not know : let us see !	*Je ne sais pas : voyons !*
11. I am so cold I cannot wait.	*J'ai si froid que je ne puis attendre.*

F

12. Come with me. Are you hungry too ? — *Venez avec moi. Avez-vous faim aussi ?*
13. No, but I'm thirsty. — *Non, mais j'ai soif.*
14. I will give you something to drink. — *Je vous donnerai à boire.*

III

1. The princess is very beautiful. — *La princesse est très belle.*
2. Let us take a walk. — *Allons-nous promener.*
3. You are too idle. — *Vous êtes trop paresseux.*
4. Do not say so, please ! — *Ne dites pas cela, je vous en prie !*
5. Is it true that she sings ? — *Est-il vrai qu'elle chante ?*
6. Yes, like a nightingale. — *Oui, comme un rossignol.*
7. Shall we go into the house ? — *Entrerons-nous dans la maison ?*
8. Not yet ; wait a moment. — *Pas encore ; attendez un moment.*
9. The weather is very mild. — *Le temps est fort doux.*
10. Go home ! — *Allez chez vous !*
11. Do you think it will rain ? — *Croyez-vous qu'il pleuvra ?*
12. Yes, certainly ; to-day or to-morrow. — *Oui sans doute ; aujourd'hui ou demain.*

IV

1. Do you love each other ? — *Vous aimez-vous l'un l'autre ?*
2. I think so. — *Je crois que oui.*
3. I had headache yesterday. — *J'ai eu mal à la tête hier.*
4. She came at twelve o'clock. — *Elle est venue à midi.*
5. Isn't it a dog I hear ? — *N'est-ce pas un chien que j'entends ?*
6. Yes, you hear it barking. — *Oui, vous l'entendez aboyer.*
7. How is your brother ? — *Comment se porte monsieur votre frère ?*
8. He is an imaginary invalid. — *C'est un malade imaginaire.*
9. Has he a good constitution then ? — *Est-il donc d'un fort tempérament ?*
10. He seems to be very well. — *Il a l'air bien portant.*
11. Yes, for a blind man. — *Ah oui, pour un aveugle.*
12. How unhappy he is ! — *Qu'il est malheureux !*
13. No, not at all ! — *Non, point du tout !*
14. Everything happens as I could wish. — *Tout m'arrive à souhait.*

15. I will do as you wish.   *Je ferai ce que vous voudrez.*
16. My heart is entirely yours.   *Mon cœur est tout à vous.*

V

1. You are right.   *Vous avez raison.*
2. I saw him yesterday.   *Je l'ai vu hier.*
3. Do not make a noise.   *Ne faites pas de bruit.*
4. Remember your friends.   *Souvenez-vous de vos amis.*
5. We go there every day.   *Nous y allons tous les jours.*
6. Where are its little ones?   *Où sont ses petits?*
7. I have not seen them.   *Je ne les ai pas vus.*
8. What's to be done? They are dying of hunger.   *Que faire? Ils meurent de faim.*
9. Do you know this child?   *Connaissez-vous cet enfant?*
10. I knew he was blind.   *Je savais qu'il était aveugle.*
11. How old is he?   *Quel âge a-t-il?*
12. He will be eight to-morrow.   *Il aura huit ans demain.*
13. Who frightens you?   *Qui vous fait peur?*
14. I heard a cry.   *J'ai entendu un cri.*

VI

1. Have you any pear-trees?   *Est-ce que vous avez des poiriers?*
2. Yes, we have several.   *Oui, nous en avons plusieurs.*
3. They were formerly very fertile.   *Ils étaient autrefois très fertiles.*
4. I see they have grown old.   *Je vois qu'ils ont vieilli.*
5. I have just heard the bees.   *Je viens d'entendre les abeilles.*
6. There is the honeycomb.   *Voilà le rayon de miel.*
7. Honey is delicious.   *Le miel est délicieux.*
8. Come and hear the birds sing.   *Venez entendre chanter les oiseaux.*
9. I have a great temptation to do so.   *J'en suis bien tenté.*
10. But I am a little tired.   *Mais je suis un peu fatigué.*
11. Sit down here for a moment.   *Asseyez-vous ici un moment.*
12. That is enough for me.   *Il ne m'en faut pas davantage.*

VII

1. Have you seen the peacock spread his tail?   *Avez-vous vu le paon faire la roue?*
2. I must look for him.   *Il faudra que je le cherche.*

3. I have just seen him in the grove. — Je viens de le voir dans le bosquet.

4. I fear we shall not find him. — Je crains que nous ne le trouvions pas.

5. How handsome he is! — Comme il est beau!

6. But his cry is not melodious. — Mais son cri n'est pas mélodieux.

7. What do you mean? — Que voulez-vous dire?

8. It's hideous, so to speak. — C'est hideux, pour ainsi dire.

9. The first time I heard it, it quite frightened me. — La première fois que je l'ai entendu, j'ai eu une belle peur.

VIII

1. Oh! you have a mirror. — Eh bien! vous avez un miroir.

2. Are you surprised to see it there? — Êtes-vous surpris de l'y voir?

3. No; I spoke jokingly. — Non; je parlais en raillant.

4. Do you like your house? — Aimez-vous votre maison?

5. Yes, more and more. — Oui, de plus en plus.

6. Just as we do. — Tout comme nous.

7. Oh! I daresay. — Je vous en réponds!

8. I come from your house. — Je viens de chez vous.

9. Very inconvenient, isn't it? — C'est bien incommode, n'est-ce pas?

10. I admit what you say. — Je conviens de ce que vous dites.

11. We are much troubled about it. — Nous en sommes au désespoir.

12. Did you not buy it? Yes! — Ne l'as-tu pas achetée? Oui!

IX

1. The acrobat has just arrived. — Le voltigeur vient d'arriver.

2. I hear he is very skilful. — { J'ai entendu dire qu'il est bien adroit; or, Il est fort adroit, à ce qu'on m'a dit.

3. He has played us a trick. — Il nous a joué un tour.

4. Many a boy has done it. — Maint garçon l'a fait.

5. He walks without a pole. — Il marche sans balancier.

6. What is the good of the pole? — À quoi bon le balancier?

7. It steadies him. — *Il le rend ferme.*

8. He must pay attention. — { *Il lui faut faire attention ;* or,
{ *Il faut qu'il fasse attention.*

9. Did you hurt yourself in falling ? — *Vous êtes-vous fait mal en tombant ?*

10. Yes, I broke my arm. — *Oui, je me suis cassé le bras.*

11. You had better be quiet. — *Vous feriez mieux de rester tranquille.*

12. I will only amuse myself. — *Je ne ferai que m'amuser.*

X

1. Look at the butterfly fluttering about. — *Voilà le papillon qui voltige.*

2. He is quite a beau. — *C'est un vrai petit-maître.*

3. He is not worth much. — *Il ne vaut pas beaucoup.*

4. Every one is worth something. — *Chacun vaut son prix.*

5. Do you like flowers ? — *Aimez-vous les fleurs ?*

6. Yes ; nothing gives me more pleasure. — *Oui ; rien ne me donne plus de plaisir.*

7. Have you any in your garden ? — *En avez-vous dans votre jardin ?*

8. I want some sadly. — *J'en ai grande envie.*

9. There are children running — *Voilà des enfants courant*

10. To catch the lovely butterfly. — *Pour prendre le beau papillon.*

11. Will they be able to catch it ? — *Pourra-t-on le prendre ?*

12. I hope not. — *J'espère que non.*

XI

1. When you are asked a question, — *Quand on vous demande quelque chose,*

2. You must answer at once. — *Il faut répondre aussitôt.*

3. Did you see the viper in the wood ? — *As-tu vu la vipère dans le bois ?*

4. Yes, it has hurt me. — *Oui, elle m'a blessé.*

5. It is only a little pricking. — *Ce n'est qu'une petite piqûre.*

6. No, but it is poisonous. — *Non, mais elle est venimeuse.*

7. I hate vipers and snakes. — *Moi, je déteste les vipères et les serpents.*

8. A leech's bite is quite different. — *La morsure d'une sangsue est bien différente.*

9. The leech is a good doctor. — *La sangsue est bon médecin.*

XII

1. Were you in Paris two days ago? — *Avez-vous été à Paris il y a deux jours ?*
2. Yes, at the Hotel d'Angleterre. — *Oui, à l'hôtel d'Angleterre.*
3. Did they give you a comfortable room? — *Vous a-t-on donné une bonne chambre ?*
4. They entertained us very well. — *On nous a fort bien traité.*
5. Where do you live now? — *Où demeurez-vous à présent ?*
6. We are here for the summer. — *Nous demeurons ici durant l'été.*
7. Please shut the door. — *Fermez la porte, s'il vous plaît.*
8. Shall I lock it? — *La fermerai-je à clef ?*
9. Yes ; double-lock it. — *Oui, à double tour.*
10. It's all the same to me. — *Cela m'est égal.*
11. I hear my father calling me. — *J'entends mon père qui m'appelle.*

XIII

1. What a lovely cat! — *Quel beau chat !*
2. Your sister must come and see it. — *Il faut que votre sœur vienne le voir.*
3. Where will it be the day after to-morrow? — *Où sera-t-il après-demain ?*
4. It will be at our house. — *Il sera chez nous.*
5. Have you looked for the rats? — *As-tu cherché les rats ?*
6. I've looked for them everywhere. — *Je les ai cherchés partout.*
7. What is his name? — *Comment s'appelle-t-il ?*
8. We have called him "Grim." — *Nous l'avons nommé " Grim."*
9. He comes at the right time. — *Il vient au bon moment.*
10. How many rooms are there? — *Combien de chambres y a-t-il ?*
11. He'll finish them off! — *Il leur donnera le coup de grâce !*

XIV

1. Where is Truth found ?	*Où se trouve la Vérité ?*
2. Seek, and you will find it.	*Cherchez-la, et vous la trouverez.*
3. Do that without my telling you.	*Faites cela sans que je vous le dise.*
4. You will make me blush.	*Vous me ferez rougir.*
5. No one will see you.	*Personne ne vous verra.*
6. I am very sorry for it !	*J'en suis bien fâché !*
7. I see her coming.	*Je la vois venir (or, qui vient).*

XV

1. What does that mean ?	*Que veut dire cela ?*
2. You fatigue me with your cries.	*Vous me fatiguez avec vos cris.*
3. I was only singing.	*Je ne faisais que chanter.*
4. What do you think of the raven ?	*Que pensez-vous du corbeau ?*
5. He is a very noisy bird.	*C'est un oiseau très bruyant.*
6. Think of what you say.	*Pensez à ce que vous dites.*
7. I always do.	*Je le fais toujours.*
8. The bullfinch died to-day.	*Le bouvreuil est mort aujourd'hui.*
9. How beautifully he sang !	*Qu'il chantait bien !*
10. Poor bird ! they forgot to feed him !	*Pauvre oiseau ! on a oublié de le nourrir !*

XVI

1. Are you afraid of bears ?	*Craignez-vous les ours ?*
2. I have never seen any in a forest.	*Je n'en ai jamais vu dans une forêt.*
3. Can they be tamed easily ?	*Peut-on les apprivoiser sans difficulté ?*
4. Yes, if you go the right way to work.	*Oui, si vous vous y prenez bien.*
5. I dare not offer you one.	*Je n'ose vous en offrir.*
6. Would you accept it ?	*Voudriez-vous l'accepter ?*
7. No ! many thanks to you !	*Non ! tout en vous remerciant !*
8. You are joking.	*Vous voulez rire.*
9. What news is there ?	*Que dit-on de nouveau ?*
10. Oh, great news !	*On dit de grandes nouvelles !*
11. Tell me what you have heard.	*Dites-moi ce que vous avez appris.*

12. The lions and panthers are quarrelling. — *Les lions et les panthères sont en querelle.*

13. They will soon come to blows. — *Ils en viendront bientôt aux coups.*

14. Better be silent than lie. — *Il vaut mieux se taire que de mentir.*

XVII

1. How old is your monkey ? — *Quel âge a votre singe ?*
2. He is still quite young. — *Il est encore tout jeune.*
3. He is only three. — *Il n'a que trois ans.*
4. Is he very clever ? — *Est-il fort habile ?*
5. He can throw a somersault. — *Il sait faire le saut périlleux.*
6. Can you show the magic lantern ? — *Savez-vous montrer la lanterne magique ?*
7. Yes, if you will close the shutters. — *Oui, si vous voulez bien fermer les volets.*
8. I have seen nothing like it. — *Je n'ai jamais vu rien de pareil.*
9. Nor I either. — *Ni moi non plus.*
10. She dresses in French style. — *Elle s'habille à la française.*
11. But she is English, isn't she ? — *Mais elle est Anglaise, n'est-ce pas ?*
12. Yes, and very pretty too. — *Oui, et elle est très-jolie.*
13. She makes the most of her height. — *Elle se plaît à étaler sa belle taille.*
14. She has no occasion to do that. — *Elle n'a que faire de cela.*

XVIII

1. Is she an only daughter ? — *Est-elle fille unique ?*
2. Yes, and a little spoiled. — *Oui, et un peu gâtée.*
3. What a pity, isn't it ? — *Quel dommage, n'est-ce pas ?*
4. You speak sensibly. — *Vous parlez raison.*
5. Is she a person of good manners ? — *Sait-elle vivre ?*
6. No, she "shuts up" everybody. — *Non, elle donne le paquet à tout le monde.*
7. She makes herself quite hated. — *Elle se fait détester.*
8. She will need discipline. — *Il lui faudra la discipline.*
9. What do you complain of ? — *De quoi vous plaignez-vous ?*
10. There is nothing for her but trouble. — *Il ne lui reste que la peine.*

11. You had better stay here.	*Vous feriez mieux de rester ici.*
12. Do not get angry.	*Ne vous mettez pas en colère.*
13. I fear she is coming.	*Je crains qu'elle ne vienne.*
14. You will bring trouble on yourself.	*Vous vous attirerez des malheurs.*
15. God forbid!	*A Dieu ne plaise!*

XIX

1. Now, you fellows, come along!	*Venez, vous autres!*
2. Which way shall we go?	*Par où irons-nous?*
3. We won't tell any one.	*Nous ne le dirons à personne.*
4. I think I hear them coming.	*Je crois les entendre venir.*
5. Speak low and go ahead.	*Parlez bas et marchez droit.*
6. What game shall we play at?	*A quel jeu jouerons-nous?*
7. Let us play at whist.	*Jouons au whist.*

XX

1. The boys were very cruel.	*Les garçons ont été bien cruels.*
2. As for the poor partridge, it died.	*Quant à la pauvre perdrix, elle est morte.*
3. Considering their youth, 1 · will not punish them severely.	*Attendu leur jeunesse, je ne les punirai pas sévèrement.*
4. In acting thus you are wrong.	*En agissant ainsi vous avez tort.*
5. They can neither read nor write.	*Ils savent ni lire ni écrire.*
6. We shall lose all unless you help us.	*Nous perdrons tout, à moins que vous ne nous aidiez.*
7. Let us wait here till they come.	*Attendons ici qu'ils viennent.*
8. Do something to bring him.	*Faites en sorte qu'il vienne.*
9. He often reads while walking.	*Il lit souvent en se promenant.*
10. Is it Spanish he is reading?	*Est-ce de l'espagnol qu'il lit?*
11. Is he a scholar? Yes.	*Est-ce qu'il est savant? Oui, il l'est.*

VOCABULARY

ABBREVIATIONS

Parts of Speech—
  adj., adjective.
  adv., adverb.
  conj., conjunction.
  interj., interjection.
  n., noun.
  prep., preposition.
  pron., pronoun.
  vb. or v., verb.
Cases—
  nom., nominative.
  acc., accusative.
  gen., genitive.
  dat., dative.
Numbers—
  s., singular.
  pl., plural.

Genders—
  m., masculine.
  f., feminine.
Verbs—
  tr., transitive.
  n., neuter.
  ref., reflexive.
Moods—
  ind., indicative.
  subj., subjunctive.
  cond., conditional.
Tenses—
  pres., present.
  pret., preterite.
  fut., future.

L. placed next to the word in the Vocabulary stands for LATIN, and is immediately followed by the Latin word or words from which the French is derived. An asterisk (*) denotes that the word is not classical Latin.

I

Compère, L. cum and patrem, m., *companion* (see note)

et, L. et, conj., *and*

son, sa, L. suum, adj., *his, her, its*

ami, L. amicum, m., *friend*

aller, L. ambulare, ir. v., *go*

à, L. ad and a (b), prep., *to, at*

pied, L. pedem, m., *foot* (à pied = *on foot*)

tout, L. totum, pl. tous, adj., *every, all*

deux, L. duos, num. adj., *two*

ville, L. villam, f., *town*

prochaine, L. propium, adj., *near, neighbouring*

trouver, L. turbare, tr. v., *find*

sur, L. super, prep., *on, upon*

chemin, L. caminum,* m., *road, way, path*

bourse, L. bursam,* f., *purse*

louis, m., *a gold coin, louis*

plein, L. plenum, adj., *full*

empocher (German origin, Anglo-Saxon pocca), tr. v., *put in one's pocket*

aussitôt, L. see note, adv., *immediately*

air, L. aërem, m., *air*

content, L. contentum, adj., *satisfied, pleased*

lui (note, l. 12), pron. dat. of il, *to him*

dire, L. dicere, tr. v., *say*

pour, L. pro, adv., *for*

bon, L. bonum, adj., *good;* also noun m., *good*

aubaine (see note), f., *windfall*

non, L. non, adv., *no, not*

répondre, L. respondēre, n. v., *answer*

froidement, from froid, L. frigidum, adv., *coldly*

est, L. est, 3d p. s. pr. ind. of être, *is*

bien, L. bene, adv., *well*

moi, L. mihi, dat. s. of je, pron., *me* (note)

différent, L. differentem, adj., *different*

souffler, L. sufflare, n. v., *blow, make a to-do*

plus, L. plus, adv., *more*

mais, L. magis, conj., *but*

en, L. in, prep., *in, on*

quitter (quitte, L. quietum), tr. v., *leave, leave quiet*

plaine, L. planam, f., *plain, open country*

voleur, from voler, L. volare, m., *thief, robber*

cacher, L. coactare, tr. v., *hide, keep close*

bois, L. boscum or buscum,* m., *wood*

voisin, L. vicinum, adj., *neighbouring*

trembler, L. tremulare, n. v., *tremble*

sans, L. sine, prep., *without*

cause, L. causam, f., *cause, reason*

sommes, L. sumus, 1st p. pl. of être, *are*

perdre, L. perdere, tr. v., *lose*

vrai, L. verum, adj., *true*

mot, L. muttum, m., *word*

toi, L. tibi, dat. s. of tu, *thou, thee*

autre, L. alterum, adj., *other, another*

chose, L. causam, f., *thing*

cela (see note), dem. pron., *that*

s'échapper (see note), ref. v., *escape*

à travers, L. ad, transversum, prep., *through, across*

taillis, from tailler, L. taleare,* *copse, coppice*

immobile, L. immobilem, adj., *motionless*

peur, L. pavorem, f., *fear, fright*

bientôt (bien, and tôt, note, l. 5), adv., *soon*

tirer (German origin, têren), tr. v., *draw out, pull*

donner, L. donare, tr. v., *give*

qui, L. qui, rel. pron., *who, which*

ne—que, L. non—quod, adv., *only*

songer, songe, L. somnium, tr. v., *think, dream*

soi, L. sibi, dat. of se, *oneself, himself*

quand, L. quando, adv., *when*

fortune, L. fortunam, f., *fortune, luck*

dans, L. de intus, prep., *into, in*

malheur, L. malum augurium, m., *misfortune*

ne—point, L. non—punctum, adv., *not at all*

II

Chacun, L. quisque, unus (see note), pron., *each one*

souvent, L. subinde, adv., *often*

connaître, L. cognoscere, tr. v., *know (a person), recognise*

défaut, L. defectum, m., *fault, defect*

convenir, L. convenire, tr. v., *confess, own*

aimer, L. amare, tr. v., *love, like*

mieux, L. melius, adv., *better*

souffrir, L. sufferre, n. v., *suffer*

véritable, L. veritabilem, adj., *real*

maux, L. malos, pl. of mal, *evils*

que, L. quam, adv., *than*

avouer, L. a, votare, tr. v., *allow, confess*

en, L. inde, gen. of il, *of it, of them, some, any*
se souvenir, L. subvenire, ref. v., *remember*
sujet, L. subjectum, m., *subject*
avoir, L. habere, aux. v., *have*
témoin, L. testimonium, m., *witness*
fait, L. factum, m., *fact, incident*
fort, L. fortem, adv., *strongly, very*
étonnant, L. ex, tonantem, adj., *astonishing*
difficile, L. difficilem, adj., *difficult*
croire, L. credĕre, tr. v., *believe*
voir, L. vidēre, tr. v., past part., vu, *see*
voici (vois ci = *see here*), prep., *here is, here are*
histoire, L. historiam, f., *history, story*
près, L. pressum, prep., *near*
soir, L. serum, m., *evening*
à l'écart, L. ex, chartam, adv., *in a lonely place*
superbe, L. superbum, adj., *proud, grand, magnificent*
prairie (pré, L. pratum), f., *meadow*
lapin (origin unknown), m., *rabbit*
s'amuser (origin uncertain), ref. v., *amuse oneself*
herbette (diminutive of herbe, L. herbam), f., *short grass*
fleurie, past part. f. of fleurir, L. florēre, *dotted with flowers*
jouer, L. jocari, n. v., *play*
colin-maillard, m., *blind man's buff*
impossible, L. impossibilem, adj., *impossible*
rien, L. rem., m., *nothing*
pourtant, L. pro, tantum, adv., *however, for all that*
feuille, L. folium, f., *leaf*
flexible, L. flexibilem, adj., *flexible, easily bent*
yeux, pl. of œil, L. oculus, m., *eye*
un, L. unum, num. adj., *one*
eux, L. illos, dat. or acc. pl., *them*
bandeau, German band, m., *band or anything over the eyes*
s'appliquer, L. applicare, ref. v., *to apply oneself, to be applied*

puis, L. post, adv., *afterwards, then*
sous, L. subtus, prep., *under*
cou, L. collum, m., *neck*
se nouer, L. nodare, ref. v., *to tie oneself, to be tied*
instant, L. instantem, m., *instant, moment*
faire, L. facĕre, tr. v., *make, do*
affaire, from à and faire, f., *affair, business*
celui, pron., *this one, that one*
que, L. quem, pron., *whom*
ruban (origin unknown), m., *riband, ribbon*
priver, L. privare, tr. v., *deprive*
lumière, L. luminaria, f., *light*
se placer (place, L. plateam), ref. v., *place or put oneself*
milieu, L. medium locum, m., *middle*
alentour (à l'entour), adv., *around*
sauter, L. saltare, n. v., *leap, jump*
danser (Old High German), n. v., *dance*
merveille, L. mirabilia, f., *wonder, marvel* (see note)
s'éloigner (loin, from L. longum), ref. v., *go away*
venir, L. venire, n. v., *come*
tour à tour, L. tornum, adv., *by turns*
queue, L. caudam, f., *tail*
ou, L. aut, conj., *or*
oreille, L. auriculam, f., *ear*
pauvre, L. pauperem, adj., *poor*
aveugle, L. aboculum,* adj., *blind*
alors (à l'ores, L. horas), adv., *then*
se retourner, L. tornare, ref. v., *turn round*
soudain, L. subitane, adv., *suddenly*
craindre, from Old French crembre, L. tremĕre, tr. v., *fear*
pot, L. potum, m., *pot* (see note)
noir, L. nigrum, adj., *black*
jeter, L. jactare, tr. v., *cast, throw*
hasard (Arabic al-sâr), m., *chance, haphazard*
patte (origin unknown), f., *paw*
troupe, L. troppum,* Low L. for turbam, f., *troop, company*

hâte (from German *hast*), f., *haste*
prendre, L. prehendĕre, tr. v., *take, catch*
vent, L. ventum, m., *wind, air*
se tourmenter, L. tormentum, ref. v., *plague oneself, toss or rush about*
vain, L. vanum, adj., *vain*
jusqu'à, L. deusque, prep., *as far as, until*
demain, L. de mane, adv., *to-morrow*
taupe, L. talpam, f., *mole*
assez, L. ad, satis, adv., *enough*
étourdi, L. extorpidum,* adj., *stunned, astonished;* also used as a noun, *madcap*
terre, L. terram, f., *earth, ground*
entendre, L. intendĕre, tr. v., *hear, understand*
bruit (origin unknown), m., *noise*
sortir, L. sortiri, n. v., *go out, come out*
réduit, L. reductum, m., *retreat, hiding-place*
se mêler, L. misculare,* ref. v., *mingle*
partie, from L. partiri, *part, game, sport*
juger, L. judicare, tr. v., *judge*
y, L. ibi, rel. adv., *there*
premier, L. primarium, adj., *first*
pas, L. passum, m., *step*
messieurs, pl. of monsieur, L. seniorem, m., *sirs, gentlemen*
conscience, L. conscientiam, f., *conscience, difficulty*
justice, L. justitiam, f., *justice*
veut, from vouloir, L. velle, and Low L. volere, tr. v., *wish, will*
notre, L. nostrum, adj., *our*
sœur, L. sororem, f., *sister*
peu, L. paucum, adv., *little*
faveur, L. favorem, f., *favour, kindness*
elle, L. illam, pron. f., *she, it*
défense, L. defensum, f., *defence, protection*
ainsi, L. in sic, conj., *so, thus*
avis, L. ad, visum, m., *advice, opinion*
avec, L. apud hoc, prep., *with*

feu, L. focum, m., *fire, warmth.*
jeu, L. jocum, m., *game, play*
mettre, L. mittĕre, tr. v., *put*
très volontiers, L. trans, voluntariis, adv., *very willingly*
cher, L. carum, adj., *dear*
nécessaire, L. necessarium, adj., *necessary*
serrer, L. serĕre, tr. v., *tie, press*
nœud, L. nodum, m., *knot, band*
pardonner, L. perdonare,* tr. .v., *pardon*
reprendre, L. reprehendĕre, n. v., *reply*
colère, L. choleram, f., *anger, wrath*
car, L. quare, conj., *for, because*
encor, L. hanc horam, adv., *still, again*

III

jeune, L. juvenem, adj., *young*
prince,·L. principem, m., *prince*
gouverneur, L. gubernatorem, m., *governor, tutor*
se promener, L. pro, minare, ref. v., *take a walk*
bocage, L. boscaticum,* m., *grove, thicket*
s'ennuyer, from ennui, L. in odio, ref. v., *to be weary*
suivre, L. sequere, tr. v., *follow*
usage, from L. usum, m., *use, custom*
profit, L. profectum, m., *profit, advantage*
grandeur, from adj. grand, L. grandem, f., *greatness*
rossignol, L. lusciniolam, m., *nightingale*
chanter, L. cantare, n. v., *sing*
feuillage (see feuille, 2), m., *foliage*
apercevoir, L. ad, percipere, tr. v., *perceive, see*
charmant, from charme, L. carmen, adj., *charming, delightful*
comme, L. quomodo, conj., *as, how*
moment, L. momentum, m., *moment, instant*
attraper, L. ad, trappam,* tr. v., *catch, entrap, get by stealth*

cage, L. caveam, f., *bird-cage*
oiseau, L. aucellam* = avicellam, m., *bird*
fuir, L. fŭgĕre, n. v., *fly, fly away*
pourquoi (pour and quoi, L. pro and quid), adv., *why*
donc, L. tunc, adv., *then*
Altesse, through Italian altezza, L. altus, f., *Highness*
se tenir, L. tenēre, ref. v., *stay, remain*
farouche, L. ferocem, adj., *wild*
solitaire, L. solitarium, adj., *lonely, alone*
tandis que, L. tamdiu, *while, whilst*
palais, L. palatium, m., *palace*
remplir, L. re, implēre, tr. v., *fill*
moineau (origin uncertain), m., *sparrow*
afin de, L. ad finem, prep., *in order to, for the purpose of*
instruire, L. instruĕre, tr. v., *instruct, teach*
jour, L. diurnum, m., *day*
devoir, L. debēre, tr. v., *owe, ought*
éprouver, L. e, probare, tr. v., *make proof, experience*
sot, L. sottum,* m., *stupid fellow, fool*
savoir, L. sapere, tr. v., *know, know how, be able*
se produire, L. producere, ref. v., *put oneself forward*
mérite, L. meritum, m., *worth, merit*
falloir, L. fallere, n. v., *be necessary, must*

IV

S'aider, L. adjutare, ref. v., *help oneself, help one another*
mutuellement, L. mutuo, adv., *mutually*
charge, L. carrico,* f., *load, burden*
léger, L. leviarium,* adj., *light*
bien, L. bene, m., *good, kindness*
frère, L. fratrem, m., *brother*
on, L. homo, indef. pron., *one, they*

soulagement, L. solatium, m., *solace, relief*
doctrine, L. doctrinam, f., *teaching*
persuader, L. persuadēre, tr. v., *persuade, enforce*
peuple, L. pŏpulum, m., *people*
Chine, prop. n., f., *China*
conter, L. computare, tr. v., *relate, tell*
trait, L. tractum, m., *action, thought, feature*
exister, L. exsistĕre, n. v., *exist, live*
perclus, L. perclusum, adj., *crippled*
ciel, L. cœlum, m., *Heaven, sky*
terminer, L. terminare, tr. v., *set bounds to, end*
leur, L. illorum, pos. adj., *their*
vie, L. vitam, f., *life*
cri, from crier, L. quiritare, m., *cry, complaint*
superflu, L. superfluum, adj., *more than necessary, useless*
pouvoir, L. potere,* n. v., *be able, can*
mourir, L. mori, n. v., *die*
paralytique, L. paralyticum, from Greek παραλυτικός, c., *one struck with palsy, paralytic*
coucher, L. collocare, tr. v., *lay down*
grabat, L. grabatum, m., *mean bed, pallet*
place, L. plateam, f., *place*
publique, L. publicum, adj., *public*
plaindre, L. plangĕre, tr. v., *pity*
nuire, L. nocēre, tr. v., *do harm, hurt*
guide, Modern Italian guida, m., *guide*
soutien, L. sustentum, m., *support, prop*
même, adv., *even*
chien, L. canem, m., *dog*
conduire,' L. conducĕre, tr. v., *guide, lead*
certain, L. certum, adj., *certain*
à tâtons, from tâter, L. taxitare,* adv., *groping along*

détour, from tourner, L. tornare, m., *turning, corner*

rue, L. rugam, f., *street*

malade, from mal, L. malum, c., *sick person,,invalid*

âme, L. animam, f., *soul, spirit*

ému, from émouvoir, L. emovēre, tr. v., *stir, affect*

tel, L. talem, adj., *such, like*

malheureux, from malheur 1, m., *unfortunate one*

vôtre, L. vostrum, pron., *yours*

unir, L. unire, tr. v., *unite, join in one*

moins, L. minus, adv., *less*

affreux, Old French afre, from High German eiver, adj., *frightful, dreadful*

hélas (hé! las, L. lassum), interj., *alas!*

ignorer, L. ignorare, tr. v., *be ignorant, not know*

puis, 1st p. s. pres. ind. of pouvoir, *can*

quoi, L. quid, pron., *what*

servir, L. servire, n. v., *be of use, serve*

misère, L. miseriam, f., *wretchedness, misery*

écouter, L. auscultare, n. v., *listen*

posséder, L. possidēre, tr. v., *possess*

jambe, L. gambam, f., *leg*

tour, L. tornum, m., *turn, trick*

vais, L. vadis from vado, 2d p. s. pres. ind. of aller, *go*

porter, L. portare, tr. v., *carry*

diriger, L. dirigēre, tr. v., *direct, guide*

mal, L. male, adv., *ill, badly*

assuré, L. assecuratum,* adj., *safe, certain*

iront, L. ire, 3d p. pl. fut. of aller, *go*

où, L. ubi, adv., *where*

sans que, L. sine, quod, conj., *without*

jamais, L. jam, magis, adv., *ever*

amitié, L. amicitiam, f., *friendship*

décider, L. decidēre, tr. v., *decide, determine*

utile, L. utilem, adj., *useful*

emploi (employer, L. implicare), *employment, post*

marcher, L. marcare,* n. v., *walk*

V

Maman, L. mammam, f., *mama, mother*

tendre, L. teneram, adj., *tender, gentle*

mère, L. matrem, f., *mother*

enfant, L. infantem, m., *child, infant*

péruvien, adj., *Peruvian, of Peru*

genou, L. genu, m., *knee*

asseoir, L. assidēre, tr. v., *seat, place*

quel, L. qualem, pron., *what, which*

animal, L. animal, m., *animal, beast*

bruyère, L. brugaria,* f., *heath, common*

petit, origin unknown, adj., *small, little*

ressembler (sembler, L. simulare), tr. v., *resemble, be like*

renard (see note), m., *fox*

fils, L. filius, m., *son*

sarigue (see note), m., *opossum*

femelle, L. femellam, f., *female*

nul, L. nullum, adj., *no, not any*

amour, L. amorem, m., *love, affection*

soin, L. sinum, m., *care, anxiety*

vigilant, L. vigilantem, adj., *watchful*

nature, L. naturam, f., *nature*

seconder, L. secundare, tr. v., *help, favour*

tendresse, L. teneritatem, f., *tenderness, fondness*

estomac, L. stomachum, m., *stomach*

poche, Anglo-Saxon pocca, f., *pouch, pocket*

profond, L. profundum, adj., *deep*

espèce, L. speciem, f., *sort, kind, species*

sac, L. saccum, m., *sack, bag*

danger, L. dominiarium,* m., *danger*

presser, L. pressare, tr. v., *press, be near*

vont, L. vadunt, 3d p. pl. pres. ind. of aller, *go*

à couvert, from couvrir, L. co-operire, adv., *under shelter*

faiblesse, from faible, formerly foible, L. flebilem, f., *weakness*

devenir, L. devenire, tr. v., *become*

frapper, Scandinavian hrappa, tr. v., *clap, strike*

main, L. manum, f., *hand*

attentif, L. attentivum, adj., *attentive, watchful*

se dresser, L. drictiare,* ref. v., *stand up, rise*

voix, L. vocem, f., *voice*

plaintif, from plaindre, adj., *pitiful, plaintive*

accourir, L. accurrĕre, n. v., *run up, hasten*

s'élancer, L. lanceam, ref. v., *throw oneself into, jump, rush*

vers, L. versum, prep., *towards, in the direction of*

chercher, L. circare, tr. v., *seek, look for*

sein, L. sĭnum, m., *bosom*

retraite, L. retractum, f., *shelter, hiding-place*

ordinaire, L. ordinarium, adj., *usual*

s'ouvrir, L. operire, ref. v., *open*

se blottir, origin unknown, ref. v., *squat, lie close*

disparaître, L. dis, parescĕre,* n. v., *disappear, vanish*

vitesse (origin unknown), f., *quickness, speed*

s'enfuir, L. inde, fugĕre, ref. v., *flee away*

emporter, L. in, portare, tr. v., *carry off, take away*

richesse, German origin, reich, f., *riches, wealth*

surprendre (sur 1, pendre 2), tr. v., *surprise*

sort, L. sortem, m., *luck, chance, fate*

contraire, L. contrarium, adj., *contrary, against*

imiter, L. imitari, tr. v., *imitate, copy*

asile, L. asylum, m., *shelter, place of refuge*

sûr, L. securum, adj., *safe, secure, sure*

VI

Jardinier, from jardin, m., *gardener*

jardin (origin Germanic, *garten*), m., *garden*

vieux, L. veclus,* adj., *old*

arbre, L. arborem, m., *tree*

stérile, L. sterilem, adj., *barren*

grand, L. grandem, adj., *large, great*

poirier, from poire, L. pirum, m., *pear-tree*

jadis, L. jam, dies, adv., *formerly, in days gone by*

fut, L. fuit, pret. of être, *was*

vieillir, from vieux, n. v., *grow old*

destin, from destiner, L. destinare, m., *fate, destiny*

ingrat, L. ingratum, adj., *ungrateful, unthankful*

abattre, from battre, L. batere, popular form of batuere, tr. v., *cut down, pull down*

matin, L. matutinum, m., *morning*

voilà (vois là = *see there*), prep., *there is, there are*

cognée, L. cuneatam, f., *axe, hatchet*

coup, L. colpum,* m., *blow, stroke*

respecter, from respect, L. respectum, tr. v., *have respect for*

âge, L. ætaticum,* m., *age*

fruit, L. fructum, m., *fruit*

chaque (see note on chacun, i.), pron. adj., *each*

année, from Merovingian Latin annata, derived from L. annus, f., *year*

mort, L. mortem, f., *death*

va, L. vadit, 3d p. s. pres. of aller, *is going*

saisir, L. of middle age, sacire, derived from High German sazjan = *place, settle,* tr. v., *seize, lay hold of*

assassiner (see note), tr. v., *assassinate, slay*

mourant, from mourir, m., *dying creature*

bienfaiteur, L. benefactorem, m., *benefactor*

couper, from coup, tr. v., *cut, cut down*

besoin (origin uncertain), m., *need, want*

gazouiller, from Provençal gasar, n. v., *warble, sing*

fois, L. vicem, f., *time;* à la fois = *at once*

centaine, from cent, L. centum, f., *hundred*

s'écrier, from crier, L. quiritare, ref. v., *cry out*

épargner (origin unknown), tr. v., *spare*

lorsque (see note), adv., *when*

femme, L. feminam, f., *wife, woman*

vient, L. venit, from venir, n. v., *comes*

s'asseoir, L. assidere, ref. v., *sit, sit down*

ombrage, L. umbraticum,* m., *shade*

rejouir, L. re, gaudere, tr. v., *gladden, make happy*

par, L. per, prep., *by, with*

doux, L. dulcis, adj., *sweet*

ramage, L. ramaticum, from ramus, m., *singing, warbling in the branches*

seul, L. solum, adj., *alone, lonely*

charmer, from charme, L. carmen, tr. v., *charm away*

ennui, L. in odio, m., *weariness*

chasser, L. captiare,* tr. v., *drive away, put to flight*

rire, L. ridere, n. v., *laugh*

requête, L. requisitam, f., *request*

second, L. secundum, adj., *second*

abeille, L. apiculam, f., *bee*

essaim, L. examen, m., *swarm*

tronc, L. truncum, m., *trunk*

arrêter, L. arrestare,* n. v., *stop*

homme, L. hominem, m., *man*

inhumain, L. inhumanum, adj., *inhuman, cruel*

laisser, L. laxare, tr. v., *leave*

miel, L. mel, m., *honey*

délicieux, L. deliciosum, adj., *delicious, delightful*

peux, L. potes, from pouvoir, *canst, art able*

vendre, L. vendere, tr. v., *sell*

rayons, from rais, L. radius, m., *honeycomb*

toucher (origin unknown), tr. v., *touch, move*

pleurer, L. plorare, n. v., *weep*

tendresse, from tendre, L. tenerum, f., *tenderness, affection*

avare, L. avarum, adj., *miserly, avaricious*

dois, L. debeo, from devoir, tr. v., *owe*

nourrir, L. nutrire, tr. v., *nourish, supply food*

jeunesse, from jeune, L. juvenem, f., *youth, young days*

quelquefois (see note), adv., *sometimes*

ouïr, L. audire, tr. v., *hear, listen to*

repos, L. re, pausare, m., *peace, quiet, repose*

daigner, L. dignari, n. v., *deign, vouchsafe*

augmenter, L. augmentare, tr. v., *increase*

aisance (origin unknown), f., *comfort, prosperity*

fleur, L. florem, f., *flower*

semer, L. seminare, tr. v., *sow, plant*

canton (origin unknown), m., *canton, district*

s'en aller (see aller), ref. v., *go away*

récompense, L. re, compensare, f., *reward, gain*

vivre, L. vivere, n. v., *live*

compter, L. computare, tr. v., *count, reckon*

reconnaissance (re and connaître), f., *gratitude*

intérêt, L. interest, m., *self-interest, regard to profit*

VII

Paon, L. pavonem, m., *peacock*

roue, L. rotam, f., *wheel* (see note)

admirer, L. admirari, tr. v., *admire*

brillant, from briller, L. beryllare,* adj., *brilliant*

plumage, from plume, L. plumam, m., *plumage*

oisons, from oie (see note), m., *goslings*

nasillard, from nasiller, derived from L. nasum, adj., *speaking through the nose, cackling*

fond, L. fundum, m., *bottom, depth*

marécage, from marais, L. mariscum,* m., *marsh, fen*

remarquer, from *marque,* a word of German origin, *mark = a sign,* tr. v., *notice, observe*

regarder, from *garder,* of German origin, n. v., *look*

plat, German origin, adj., *flat*

hideux, L. hispidosum,* adj., *hideous, ugly*

mélodieux, Greek μελωδία, adj., *melodious*

fuir, L. fugere, n. v., *fly, fly away*

chouette (see note), f., *owlet*

mal, L. malum, m., *evil, harm*

tout à coup, adv., *all at once, suddenly*

plongeon, from plonger, L. plumbicare,* m., *diver*

crier, L. quiritare, n. v., *cry, cry out*

lieue, L. leucam, f., *league*

manquer, L. adj., mancus, n. v., *fail, be wanting*

chant, L. cantum, m., *singing, song*

laid, German origin, *laid = odious,* adj., *disagreeable, ugly*

sien, from son (see note), poss. pron., *his, hers*

queue, L. caudam, f., *tail*

VIII

Élever, L. e, levare, tr. v., *bring up, rear*

village, L. villaticum,* m., *village*

revenir, L. revenire, n. v., *return, come back*

chez, L. casam, prep., *to the home of, at the home of*

miroir, from mirer, L. mirari, m., *mirror, looking-glass*

d'abord, from Netherlandic bord = edge, adv., *at first*

image, L. imaginem, f., *likeness, image*

travers, L. transversum, m., *whim*

digne, L. dignum, adj., *worthy*

être, L. esse, m., *being*

outrager, from outre, L. ultra, tr. v., *insult, outrage*

grimace (German origin), f., *grimace*

rendre, L. rendere (nasal pronunciation of reddere), tr. v., *give back, return*

dépit, L. despectum, m., *anger, vexation*

extrême, L. extremum, adj., *very great, extreme*

montrer, L. monstrare, tr. v., *show*

poing, L. pugnum, m., *fist*

menaçant, from menace, L. minaciæ, adj., *threatening*

menacer, tr. v., *threaten*

marmot (origin unknown), m., *brat*

fâcher, from Provençal fastigar, L. fastidium, tr. v., *grieve, make angry*

s'en venir, n. v., *come away*

frémir, L. fremere, n. v., *tremble, fret, fume*

battre, L. batere (batuere), tr. v., *beat, strike*

insolent, L. insolentem, adj., *insolent, impudent*

furieux, L. furiosum, adj., *raging, furious*

désespoir, from dé and espoir, L. speres, m., *despair*

devant, from de and avant, L. ab ante, prep., *before, in front of*

glace, L. glaciem, f., *looking-glass, ice*

survenir, L. supervenire, n. v., *come unexpectedly, come up* consoler, L. consolari, tr. v., *comfort, console*

embrasser, from bras, L. brachium, tr. v., *embrace, fondle*

tarir, German origin, tr. v., *dry*

pleurs, from pleurer, L. plorare, m., *tears*

doucement, from doux, L. dulcem, adv., *gently*

commencer, L. cum, initiare, n. v., *begin*

méchant, from old verb meschéoir, L. minus cadere, adj., *wicked, bad*

causer, from cause, L. causam, tr. v., *cause*

oui, L. hoc illud, adv., *yes*

à présent, L. ad presentem, adv., *now*

sourire, L. subridere, n. v., *smile*

tendre, L. tendere, tr. v., *stretch out*

société, L. societatem, f., *society, social life*

emblème, L. emblema, from Greek ἔμβλημα, m., *emblem*

IX

Grillon, L. grillus,* m., *cricket (insect)*

herbe, L. herbam, f., *grass, herb*

papillon, L. papilionem, m., *butterfly*

voltiger, from Italian volteggiare, n. v., *flutter about*

insecte, L. insectum, m., *insect*

ailé, L. alam (aile = *wing*), adj., *winged*

briller, L. beryllare,* n. v., *sparkle, glitter, shine*

vif, L. vivum, adj., *lively, smart, sprightly*

couleur, L. colorem, f., *colour*

azur, L. lazurrum,* m., *blue, azure*

pourpre, L. purpuram, m., *purple*

or, L. aurum, m., *gold*

éclater, from Old High German skleizan, which became skleitan, n. v., *sparkle, shine*

aile, L. alam, f., *wing*

beau (bel, L. bellus), f. belle, adj., *beautiful, handsome*

petit-maître, L. magistrum, m., *beau, dandy*

courir, L. currere, n. v., *run*

mien, softened form of mon, L. meum, pron., *mine*

Dame, L. dominam, f., *Dame, lady*

talent, L. talentum, m., *talent, powers*

figure, L. figuram, f., *shape, figure, form*

garde, Old High German warten = garder, f., *care, attention, protection*

ici-bas, bas, L. bassum, adv., *here below, in this world*

autant, L. aliud tantum, adv., *as well, as much*

valoir, L. valere, n. v., *be worth, be good for*

après, L. ad, pressum, prep., *after*

dont, L. de-unde, gen. of qui, pron., *of which*

envie, L. invidiam, f., *desire, fancy, envy*

chapeau, from chape, L. cappam * (note, i. 14), m., *hat*

mouchoir, from moucher, L. muccare,* m., *handkerchief*

bonnet (origin unknown), m., *cap*

vainement, L. vanâ mente, adv., *vainly, uselessly*

conquête, L. conquisitum, f., *conquest, prey*

corps, L. corpus, m., *body*

troisième, from trois, L. tres, adj., *third*

falloir, L. fallere, impers. v., *need, be necessary, must*

tant, L. tantum, adv., *so many, so much*

efforts, from forcer, L. fortiare,* m., *effort*

déchirer (German origin), tr. v., *tear, tear in pieces*

bête, L. bestiam, f., *beast, creature*

coûter, L. constare, tr. v., *cost*

monde, L. mundum, m., *world*

combien, from comme (3), and bien (1), adv., *how much, how many* heureux, from heur, L. augurium, adj., *happy*

X

Corde, L. chordam, f., *rope, string*

voltigeur, from voltiger (9), m., *vaulter, acrobat*

apprendre, L. apprendere (apprehendere), tr. v., *learn*

déjà, adv., *already*

adresse, from dresser (5), f., *skill, expertness*

force, L. fortiam,* f., *strength, force, power*

souplesse, from souple, L. supplicem, f., *suppleness, activity*

maint, Celtic maint = *magnitude*, or Old High German manag, which has become in Modern German manch, English *many*, adj., *many*

spectateur, L. spectatorem, m., *spectator, looker on*

étroit, L. strictum, adj., *narrow, strait*

s'avancer, from avant, L. abante, ref. v., *go forward*

balancier, from balance, L. bilancem, m., *balancing-pole*

libre, L. liberum, adj., *free, bold*

droit, L. directum, adj., *straight, upright*

hardi (German origin), adj., *brave, bold*

adroit, from droit (see above), *skilful*

s'élever (see 8), ref. v., *go up, rise*

descendre, L. descendere, n. v., *come down*

haut, L. altum, adv., *high;* also adj., *high, tall*

retomber, from tomber, Scandinavian tumba = *fall*, n. v., *fall back*

remonter, from mont, L. montem, n. v., *go up again*

cadence, from Italian cadenza, L. cadere, f., *cadence*

semblable, from sembler, L. simulare, adj., *like*

raser, from ras, L. rasum, tr. v., *skim, pass lightly over*

voler, L. volare, n. v., *fly*

surface, L. superfa(i)ciem, f., *top, surface*

eau, L. aquam, f., *water*

plier, L. plicare, n. v., *yield, bend*

renvoyer, from envoyer, L. (in)deviare, tr. v., *send back*

danseur, from danser (2), m., *dancer*

fier, L. ferum, adj., *proud*

pesant, from peser, L. pensare, adj., *heavy, weighty*

fatiguer, L. fatigare, tr. v., *tire, fatigue*

embarrasser, from barre, L. barram,* from Celtic bar, tr. v., *embarrass, hinder*

grâce, L. gratiam, f., *grace, elegance*

légèreté, from léger (4), f., *lightness, agility, spring*

chanceler, L. cancellare, n. v., *stagger, waver*

étendre, L. extendere, tr. v., *stretch out*

tomber, Scandinavian tumba, n. v., *fall*

se casser, L. quassare, ref. v., *break*

nez, L. nasum, m., *nose*

gens, L. gentes, m. pl., *people, persons*

règle, L. regulam, f., *rule, order*

frein, L. frenum, m., *horse's bit, restraint*

tôt, L. tot-cito, adv., *soon*

tard, L. tardum, adv., *late*

succomber, L. succumbere, n. v., *sink, give in*

vertu, L. virtutem, f., *virtue*

raison, L. rationem, f., *right, justice, reason*

loi, L. legem, f., *law*

autorité, L. auctoritatem, f., *authority*

désir, L. desiderium, m., *desire, passion*

fougueux, from Italian foga, adj., *unruly, furious, fierce, fiery*

peine, L. pœnam, f., *trouble, difficulty, pain*

gêner, L. gehenna, tr. v., *restrain, keep down, disquiet*
sûreté, L. securitatem, f., *safety*

XI

Vipère, L. viperam, f., *viper*
sangsue, L. sanguisugam, f., *leech, blood-sucker*
tuer, L. tutari, tr. v., *kill*
loin, L. longe, adv., *far*
blessure (origin uncertain), f., *wound*
sang, L. sanguinem, m., *blood*
ample, L. amplum, adj., *plentiful, ample*
nourriture, L. nutrituram, f., *nourishment, food*
cependant (see note), adv., *yet, in the meantime*
même, adj., *same*
piqûre, from Celtic pic, f., *pricking, sting*
citoyenne, L. civitadanam,* derived from civitatem (cité), f., *citizen, inhabitant*
étang, L. stagnum, m., *pond, pool*
nenni, L. non illud, adv., *by no means*
salutaire, L. salutarem, adj., *healthful, wholesome*
obtenir, L. obtinere, tr. v., *gain, obtain*
guérison, from guérir, Gothic warjan, f., *cure*
sain, L. sanum, adj., *healthy, sound*
cruel, L. crudelem, adj., *cruel*
entre, L. inter, prep., *between, among*
différence, L. differentiam, f., *difference*
remède, L. remedium, m., *remedy*
poison, L. potionem, m., *poison*
fable, L. fabulam, f., *fable*
aisément, from aise (origin unknown), adv., *easily*
s'expliquer, L. explicare, ref. v., *be explained*
satire, L. satiram, f., *satire*
critique, L. criticum, from Greek κριτικός, f., *criticism*

XII

Aventure, from avenir, L. advenire, f., *mischance, adventure*
se traiter, L. tractare, ref. v., *treat oneself*
marché, L. mercatum, m., *market, bargain*
acheter, L. ad-captare, tr. v., *buy*
pomme, L. pomum, f., *apple*
armoire, L. armarium, f., *closet, cupboard*
ranger, from rang, Old High German hring = *circle*, tr. v., *arrange, place in order*
recompter, L. re, computare, tr. v., *count again*
fermer, L. firmare, tr. v., *shut*
double, L. duplicem, adj., *double*
serrure, from serrer, L. serere, f., *lock*
visiter, L. visitare, tr. v., *visit, go to see*
folie, from fol, L. follum * (derived from follis), f., *folly*
ménager, from ménage, L. mansionaticum,* tr. v., *take care of, husband, save, keep*
quelqu'un, quelque (note, vi. 32), and un, L. unum, *some one*
pourrir, L. putrere, n. v., *rot, decay*
soupirer, L. suspirare, n. v., *sigh*
écolier, from école, L. scholam, m., *schoolboy*
maigre, L. macrum, adj., *thin, poor*
chère, L. caram,* f., *cheer, food*
découvrir, L. dis, cooperire, tr. v., *discover*
fin, L. finem, f., *end*
clef, L. clavem, f., *key*
excellent, L. excellentem, adj., *excellent*
appétit, L. appetitum, m., *appetite*
dégât, from gâter, L. vastare, m., *havoc*
périr, L. perire, n. v., *perish, come to an end*
douleur, L. dolorem, f., *grief, sorrow*

effroi, from effrayer, L. exfrigidare, m., *fright*
palpiter, L. palpitare, n. v., *pant, palpitate*
coquin (origin uncertain), m., *rogue*
pendre, L. pendere, tr. v., *hang*
se calmer, from Italian calma, ref. v., *be calm*
plaire, L. placere, tr. v., *please*
honnête, L. honestum, adj., *honest*
personne, L. personam, f., *person*
tort, L. tortum, m., *wrong*

XIII.

Angora (see note), c., *Angora (cat)*
maîtresse, from maître, L. magistrum, f., *mistress*
mets, L. missum, m., *dish, meat*
délicat, L. delicatum, adj., *dainty, delicate*
guerre, Old High German werra, f., *war*
rat, Old High German rato, m., *rat*
bonté, L. bonitatem, f., *goodness, kindness*
paresse, L. pigritiam, f., *idleness*
trotter, L. tolutare,* n. v., *trot, ramble*
partout, L. per totum, adv., *everywhere*
grenier, L. granarium, m., *granary, loft*
retirer, from tirer (German origin), tr. v., *retire, withdraw*
chat, L. catum,* m., *cat*
dormir, L. dormire, n. v., *sleep*
festin, Italian festino, m., *banquet, feast*
plusieurs, L. pluriores, adj., *several, many*
grain, L. granum, m., *grain, corn*
repas, L. repastum, m., *repast, meal*
bouger, L. bullicare, from bullire, n. v., *stir*
penser, L. pensare, n. v., *think*
orateur, L. oratorem, m., *orator*
parler, L. parabolare, n. v., *speak*
mépris, from priser, L. pretiare, m., *contempt, scorn*

applaudir, L. applaudere, n. v., *applaud, clap hands*
s'attrouper, from troupe (ii.), ref. v., *flock together*
proclamer, L. proclamare, tr. v., *proclaim*
général, L. generalem, m., *general (of an army)*
grimper (German origin), n. v., *climb up*
boisseau, L. bustellum, m., *bushel (for measuring grain)*
tribunal, L. tribunal, m., *Tribune*
brave, from Italian bravo, adj., *brave, courageous*
vengeance, from venger, L. vindicare, f., *vengeance*
grain, L. granum, m., *grain*
désormais (see note), adv., *henceforth, for the future*
las, L. lassum, adj., *tired, weary*
jurer, L. jurare, n. v., *swear*
bombance (origin uncertain), f., *feasting, banquet*
partager, from partir, L. partiri, tr. v., *share*
belliqueux, L. bellicosum, adj., *warlike*
transport, from transporter, L. transportare, m., *delight, ecstasy*
nouveau, L. novellum, adj., *new, fresh*
guerrier, from guerre, m., *warrior*
réveiller, L. re, exvigilare,* tr. v., *wake again*
celui-ci, pron., *the latter*
juste, L. justum, adj., *just, righteous*
poussière, from pousse, L. pulvis, f., *dust*
tribun, L. tribunum, m., *tribune*
soldat, Italian soldato, m., *soldier*
vite (origin uncertain), adv., *quickly*
tanière, L. taxum (origin uncertain), f., *hiding-place, den*
pousser, L. pulsare, tr. v., *push, drive*
bout, from High German bôzen, m., *end, extremity*
ennemi, L. inimicum, m., *enemy*
débonnaire (de bon aire), adj., *good-natured*
tenir, L. tenere, tr. v., *hold, have*

gagner (German origin), tr. v.,
gain

XIV

Siècle, L. sæculum, m., *age, century,
time*
humains, L. humanos, m. pl.,
men, mankind
paix, L. pacem, f., *peace*
couler, L. colare, n. v., *roll on,
pass smoothly*
pur, L. purum, adj., *pure*
serein, L. serenum, adj., *calm,
serene*
vérité, L. veritatem, f., *truth*
sincère, L. sincerum, adj., *sincere,
genuine*
retracer, L. re, tractiare, derived
from tractus, tr. v., *describe,
draw again*
secret, L. secretum, adj., *secret*
rougir, from rouge, L. rubeum,
n. v., *blush*
ne—guère (German origin), adv.,
but little, not long
durer, L. durare, n. v., *last*
criminel, L. criminalem, adj.,
criminal
débris, from briser, Old High German bristan, m., *broken remains,
ruins*
chute, from choir, L. cadere, f.,
fall
disperser, L. dispersare,* derived
from dispersus, tr. v., *scatter,
disperse*
vulgaire, L. vulgarem, m., *the
common crowd, mob*
prix, L. pretium, m., *price*
depuis, from puis, L. post, prep.,
since
sage, L. sapium, from sapiens,
adj., *wise (man)*
retrouver, from trouver, L. turbare, tr. v., *find again*
parfois, from par (vi.) and fois
(vi.), adv., *at times, sometimes*
entier, L. integrum, adj., *whole,
perfect*

XV

Bouvreuil, L. bovariolum,* m.,
bullfinch

corbeau, L. corvellum, m., *raven*
habiter, L. habitare, n. v., *live,
dwell*
logis, L. laubiam,* m., *house,
dwelling-place*
mari, L. maritum, m., *husband*
ménage, L. mansionaticum,* m.,
family, household
cesse, from cesser, L. cessare, f.,
generally used only with sans—
sans cesse, *unceasingly*
demander, L. demandare, tr. v.,
ask for, demand
pain, L. panem, m., *bread*
rôti, from rôtir, High German
rostjan, m., *roast meat*
fromage, L. formaticum,* m.,
cheese
se presser (see v.), ref. v., *hasten,
make haste*
se taire, L. tacere, ref. v., *be silent,
be quiet*
timide, L. timidum, adj., *timid*
aussi, L. aliud sic, adv., *so*
oublier, L. oblitare,* from oblitus,
tr. v., *forget*
louer, L. laudare, tr. v., *praise*
harmonie, L. harmoniam, f.,
harmony
moindre, L. minorem, adj., *less*
auge, L. alveum, f., *trough*
faim, L. famem, f., *hunger, star-
vation*
las, L. lassum, interj., *alas!*
certes, L. certis, adv., *certainly,
indeed*
dommage, L. damnum, m., *pity,
loss*

XVI

Valeureux, from valeur, L. val-
orem, adj., *valorous, brave*
lion, L. leonem, m., *lion*
roi, L. regem, m., *king*
immense, L. immensum, adj.,
unmeasured, immense
désirer, L. desiderare, tr. v.,
desire, covet
conquérir, L. conquirere, tr. v.,·
conquer
forêt, L. forestam,* f., *forest*

héritage, from hériter, L. hereditare,* m., *estate, inheritance*

léopard, L. leopardum, m., *leopard*

attaquer (origin uncertain), tr. v., *attack*

panthère, L. pantheram, f., *panther*

ours, L. ursum, m., *bear*

juste, L. juste, adv., *rightly (exactly)*

cour, L. chortem, f., *court, courtyard, domain*

comment, from comme, L. quomodo, adv., *how*

monarque, μόναρχος, m., *monarch, one who rules alone*

habile, L. habilem, adj., *skilful, clever*

prétexte, L. prætextum, m., *pretence, pretext*

bonneur, L. honorem, m., *honour*

députer, L. deputare, tr. v., *depute*

ambassadeur, L. ambactus (note), m., *ambassador*

admettre, L. admittere, tr. v., *admit*

audience, L. audientiam, f., *audience*

vanter, L. vanitare, tr. v., *praise, extol, commend*

prudence, L. prudentiam, f., *prudence*

douceur, L. dulcorem, f., *sweetness, gentleness*

bienfaisance, L. beneficentiam, f., *beneficence, bounty*

nom, L. nomen, m., *name*

proposer, from poser, L. pausare, tr. v., *propose*

alliance, from allier, L. alligare, f., *alliance*

exterminer, L. exterminare, tr. v., *put an end to*

méconnaître, from mes, L. minus and connaitre (ii.), tr. v., *not acknowledge, slight, disown*

puissance, from puissant, L. possentem, derived from posse, f., *power*

accepter, L. acceptare, tr. v., *accept, agree*

dès, L. de ipso (tempore), prep., *from*

lendemain (see note), m., *the next day*

héros, L. heros, m., *hero*

frontière, L. fronteria,* derived from frontem, f., *frontier, border*

manger, L. manducare, tr. v., *eat*

pays, L. pagensem, from pagus, m., *country*

fixer, from fixe, L. fixum, tr. v., *fix, settle*

borne, L. bodinam,* f., *boundary, landmark*

querelle, L. querelam, f., *quarrel, complaint*

léser, from lése, L. læsum, tr. v., *hurt, wrong, injure*

denture, from dent, L. dentem, f., *set of teeth*

prouver, L. probare, tr. v., *prove*

bref, L. breve, adv., *in short*

trépas, L. trans passum, m., *death*

contre, L. contra, prep., *against*

barrière, Low L. barra, from Celtic bar, f., *barrier*

état, L. statum, m., *state*

XVII

Esprit, L. spiritum, m., *spirit, wit*

prose, L. prosam, f., *prose*

vers, L. versum, m., *verse*

style, L. stylum, m., *style*

pompeux, L. pomposum, adj., *pompous, showy*

toujours, tout and jour, adv., *always*

admirable, L. admirabilem, adj., *admirable, marvellous*

tâcher, L. tascam,* n. v., *try*

clair, L. clarum, adj.,, *clear, perspicuous*

lanterne, L. lanternam, f., *lantern*

magique, L. magiam, adj., *magic*

singe, L. simium, m., *monkey*

attirer, from tirer (German origin), tr. v., *attract*

concours, L. concursum, m., *concourse, crowd*

élastique, Greek ἐλαστικός, adj., *elastic*

saut, L. saltum, m., *leap*

périlleux, L. periculosum, adj., *dangerous*

cordon, from corde, L. chordam, m., *string*

soutenir, L. sustinere, tr. v., *hold up*

fixe, L. fixum, adj., *fixed, steady*

d'aplomb, L. ad, plumbum, adv., *upright*

long, L. longum, m., *length*

exercice,|L. exercitium, m., *exercise*

à la, *after the fashion, in style*

prussien, adj., *Prussian*

cabaret (origin unknown), m., *public-house*

rester, L. restare, n. v., *stay, remain*

fête, L. festa, f., *feast, festival*

liberté, L. libertatem, f., *liberty, freedom*

rassembler, L. re, assimulare, tr. v., *collect together*

divers, L. diversum, adj., *various, different*

rencontrer, from re, en, contre, tr. v., *meet*

poulet, from poule, L. pullam, m., *chicken*

dindon, coq d'Inde (note), m., *turkey*

pourceau, L. porcellum, m., *little pig*

file, L. filum, f., *file, row*

entrer, L. intrare, n. v., *enter, come in*

spectacle, L. spectaculum, m., *show*

gratis, L. gratis, adv., *for nothing, gratis*

porte, L. portam, f., *door*

argent, L. argentum, m., *money*

apporter, L. ad, portare, tr. v., *bring*

volet, from voler, L. volare, m., *shutter*

discours, L. discursum, m., *discourse, speech*

exprès, L. expressum, adv., *on purpose*

préparer, L. preparare, tr. v., *prepare*

auditoire, L. auditorium, m., *audience*

morceau, L. morsellum,* m., *piece, bit*

vraiment, L. verâ mente, adv., *truly*

oratoire, L. oratorium, adj., *oratorical*

bâiller, L. badaculare, n. v., *gape*

succès, L. successum, m., *success*

verre, L. vitrum, m., *glass*

peindre, L. pingere, tr. v., *paint*

gouverner, L. gubernare, tr. v., *manage, guide*

pareil, L. pariculum,* from par, adj., *equal, like*

soleil, L. soliculum, from sol, m., *sun*

gloire, L. gloriam, f., *glory*

présentement, L. presenti mente, adv., *now*

lune, L. lunam, f., *moon*

naissance, L. nascentiam, f., *birth*

nuit, L. noctem, f., *night*

écarquiller (origin uncertain), n. v., *open (the eyes or legs) wide*

appartement, L. appartiamentum,* m., *room, floor*

mur, L. murum, m., *wall*

foi, L. fidem, f., *faith*

distinguer, L. distinguere, n. v., *distinguish*

pendant, L. pendente (re), prep., *during*

moderne, L. modernum, adj., *modern*

éloquemment, L. eloquenti mente, adv., *eloquently*

se lasser, L. lassare, ref. v., *grow tired*

éclairer, L. exclarare, tr. v., *light up*

XVIII

Linotte, from lin, L. linum, f., *linnet*

adorer, L. adorare, tr. v., *adore, worship*

selon, L. sub longum, prep., *according to*

unique, L. unicum, adj., *only, sole, unique*

mariage, L. maritaticum,* m., *marriage*

linot (see above), m., *linnet*

fou, L. follum, adj., *fond, foolish*

témoignage, from témoin, L. testimonium, m., *evidence, proof*

inventer, L. inventare* from supine of invenire, tr. v., *invent, discover*

épuiser, from puits, L. puteus, tr. v., *drain, exhaust*

avantage, from avant, L. abante, m., *advantage, honour*

phénix, Greek φοῖνιξ, m., *phenix*

suffisant, L. sufficientem, adj., *self-sufficient*

trancher (origin unknown), n. v., *set up for*

important, L. importantem, m., *person of importance*

persifler, from siffler, L. sifilare,* tr. v., *quiz, banter*

mésange (origin uncertain), f., *titmouse*

roitelet, from roi, L. regem, m., *wren*

paquet, L. paccum,* m., *packet, bundle*

haïr (German origin), tr. v., *hate*

voisinage, from voisin, L. vicinum, m., *neighbourhood*

modeste, L. modestum, adj., *modest*

surtout, L. super, totum, adv., *above all*

concevoir, L. concipere, tr. v., *conceive, understand*

don, L. donum, m., *gift*

qualité, L. qualitatem, f., *quality, accomplishment*

partage, from partir, L. partiri, m., *share, portion*

feindre, L. fingere, tr. v., *pretend, feign*

pour que, L. pro, quod, conj., *so that*

davantage, from de and avantage, adv., *more*

merle, L. merulam, m., *blackbird*

mois, L. mensem, m., *month*

alarme, Italian all'arme, f., *alarm, fright*

brûler, L. perustulare, from ustus, n. v., *burn*

voyager, from voyage, L. viaticum, n. v., *travel*

partir, L. partiri, n. v., *set out, start*

malgré, from mal, L. malum and gré, L. gratum, prep., *in spite of*

larme, L. lacrymam, f., *tear*

à peine, L. poenam, adv., *scarcely, hardly*

personnage, from personne (xii.), m., *personage*

pivert, from pic, L. picum, m., *woodpecker*

se moquer (origin unknown), ref. v., *laugh at, ridicule*

fausset, from faux, L. falsus, m., *shrill treble, falsetto*

plaisanterie, from plaire, L. placere, f., *joke, jest*

bec, L. beccum, m., *bill* (of a bird), *beak*

plumer, L. plumare, tr. v., *pluck, strip (of feathers)*

persifleur (see persifler above), m., *banterer, mocker*

pie, L. picam, f., *magpie*

dégoûter, L. degustare, tr. v., *put out of conceit*

métier, L. ministerium, m., *trade, roll*

railleur, from railler, L. radiculare,* m., *joker, jeerer*

vanité, L. vanitatem, f., *vanity*

chanteur, from chanter, L. cantare, m., *singer*

fauvette, from German falb, f., *warbler*

guérir, from German warjan, tr. v., *cure*

erreur, L. errorem, m., *mistake, error*

poli, L. politum, adj., *polite, courteous*

adversité, L. adversitatem, f., *adversity*

leçon, L. lectionem, f., *lesson*

pu, past part. of pouvoir (iv.), *been able*

XIX

Chaud, L. cal(i)dum, adj., *hot*

guenon (origin unknown), f., *ape*

mauricaud (see note), adj., *African*

gravement, L. gravi mente, adv., *gravely, seriously*

courber, from courbe, L. curvum, tr. v. *bend, curve*

échine (German origin), f., *backbone, spine*

deviner, L. divinare, n. v., *guess*

ris, L. risum, m., *laugh, laughter*

saut, L. saltum, m., *jump, leap*

gambade, Italian gambata, f., *gambol*

se présenter, L. presentare, ref. v., *appear*

joyeux, L. gaudiosum, adj., *joyous, merry*

aspect, L. aspectum, m., *look, appearance*

continuer, L. continuare, tr. v., *go on with*

se rassurer, from assurer, L. assecurare,* ref. v., *take courage again*

particulier, L. particularem, m., *private person*

s'associer, L. associare, ref. v., *join in*

dignité, L. dignitatem, f., *dignity*

fantaisie, Greek φαντασία, f., *fancy*

philosophie, Greek φιλοσοφία, f., *philosophy, love of wisdom*

égal, L. æqualem, adj., *equal*

prier, L. precare, tr. v., *beg, pray*

enchanter, L. incantare, tr. v., *enchant*

jovial, Italian giovale, adj., *jovial, jolly*

se remettre, L. remittere, ref. v., *set to again*

couler, L. colare, n. v., *flow, trickle*

griffe, German grif, f., *claw*

royal, L. regalem, adj., *royal*

compagnon, L. cum, panis, m., *companion*

semblant, L. simulationem, m., *pretence, show*

s'excuser, L. excusare, ref. v., *make excuse*

dent, L. dentem, f., *tooth*

XX

Fermier, from ferme, L. firmum, m., *farmer*

gentil, L. gentilem, adj., *pretty*

espiègle (see note), adj., *a little mischievous, frolicsome*

gâter, L. vastare, tr. v., *spoil*

nid, L. nidum, m., *nest*

enclos, L. inclusum, m., *enclosure*

perdreau, from perdrix, L. perdrix, m., *young partridge*

voleter, L. volitare, n. v., *flutter*

joie, L. gaudia, f., *joy*

bambin, Italian bambino, m., *baby*

s'éparpiller, from L. papilio, ref. v., *spread about*

famille, L. familiam, f., *family, brood*

perdrix, L. perdrix, f., *partridge*

traîner, tr. v., *drag, hang (a wing)*

appeler, L. appellare, tr. v., *call*

tourner, L. tornare, n. v., *turn*

s'approcher, L. appropiare, ref. v., *come near*

couvée, from couver, L. cubare, f., *covey, brood*

garder (German origin), tr. v., *keep*

treizième, from treize, L. tredecim, adj., *thirteenth*

aîné, L. ante natum, m., *eldest son*

doigt, L. digitum, m., *finger*

mouiller, L. moliare, tr. v., *wet, soak*

parbleu (see note), int., *zounds, forsooth*

si, L. sic., adv., *yes, so*

céder, L. cedere, tr. v., *give up*

propos, L. propositum, m., *words*

patient, L. patientem, adj., *patient, gentle*

disputer, L. disputare, tr. v., *dispute*

cadet, L. capitellum,* from caput, m., *younger brother*

riposter, Italian riposta, n. v., *reply smartly*

recommencer, L. re, cum, initiare, n. v., *begin again*

couvrir, L. coöperire, tr. v., *cover*

autour de, from tour, L. turrim, prep., *around*

passer, L. passare,* from passum, n. v., *pass by*

champ, L. campum, m., *field*

sanguinaire, L. sanguiuarium, adj., *of blood, sanguinary*

accourir, L. accurrere, n. v., *run up*

discorde, L. discordia, f., *disagreement, quarrel*

innocent, L. innocentem, adj., *innocent, harmless*

expirer, L. exspirare, n. v., *expire, die*

triste, L. tristem, adj., *sad, grievous*

IRREGULAR VERBS

Remember that there are FIVE Principal Parts in a French Verb, and knowing these, you can form, almost always, the rest of the Verb.

PRINCIPAL PARTS.	TENSE FORMED.	HOW FORMED.
Infinitive Mood	{ Future Indic. . { Pres. Condit. .	{ Add Pres. of avoir. { Add Imp. of avoir.
Present Participle	{ Plural of Pres. Ind. { Imperfect Ind. { Present Subj. .	{ Change ant into ons, etc. { ,, ,, ais. { ,, ,, e.
Past Participle	{ All Compound { Tenses .	{ Using the Auxiliary Verb avoir ; or, for Reflexive Verbs and Verbs of motion, être.
Present Indic.	Imperative Mood	{ Drop 1st person sing., and the subjective pronouns.
Preterite Indic.	Imp. Subj.	{ Change the last letter into sse.

INF.	PRES. PART.	PAST PART.	PRES. IND.	PRET. IND.
aller (*go*),	allant,	allé,	vais,	allai.
asseoir (*seat*),	asseyant,	assis,	assieds,	assis.
conduire (*conduct*),	conduisant,	conduit,	conduis,	conduisis.
connaître (*know*),	connaissant,	connu,	connais,	connus.
conquérir (*conquer*),	conquérant,	conquis,	conquiers,	conquis.
courir (*run*),	courant,	couru,	cours,	courus.
couvrir (*cover*),	couvrant,	couvert,	couvre,	couvris.
craindre (*fear*),	craignant,	craint,	crains,	craignis.
croire (*believe*),	croyant,	cru,	crois,	crûs.
dire (*say*),	disant,	dit,	dis,	dis.
disparaître (*disappear*),	disparaissant,	disparu,	disparais,	disparus.
émouvoir (*move*),	émouvant,	ému,	émeus,	émus.

Inf.	Pres. Part.	Past Part.	Pres. Ind.	Pret. Ind.
faire (*make*),	faisant,	fait,	fais,	fis.
falloir (*need*),		fallu,	il faut,	il fallut.
feindre (*sham*),	feignant,	feint,	feins,	feignis.
fuir (*flee*),	fuyant,	fui,	fuis,	fuis.
instruire (*instruct*),	instruisant,	instruit,	instruis,	instruisis.
mettre (*put*),	mettant,	mis,	mets,	mis.
mourir (*die*),	mourant,	mort,	meurs,	mourus.
nuire (*hurt*),	nuisant,	nui,	nuis,	nuisis.
ouvrir (*open*),	ouvrant,	ouvert,	ouvre,	ouvris.
peindre (*paint*),	peignant,	peint,	peins,	peignis.
plaindre (*complain*),	plaignant,	plaint,	plains,	plaignis.
plaire (*please*),	plaisant,	plu,	plais,	plus.
pouvoir (*be able*),	pouvant,	pu,	peux,	pus.
prendre (*take*),	prenant,	pris,	prends,	pris.
rire (*laugh*),	riant,	ri,	ris,	ris.
savoir (*know*),	sachant,	su,	sais,	sus.
sortir (*go out*),	sortant,	sorti,	sors,	sortis.
souffrir (*suffer*),	souffrant,	souffert,	souffre,	souffris.
suivre (*follow*),	suivant,	suivi,	suis,	suivis.
se taire (*be silent*),	taisant,	tu,	tais,	tus.
tenir (*hold*),	tenant,	tenu,	tiens,	tins.
valoir (*be worth*),	valant,	valu,	vaux,	valus.
venir (*come*),	venant,	venu,	viens,	vins.
vivre (*live*),	vivant,	vécu,	vis,	vécus.
voir (*see*),	voyant,	vu,	vois,	vis.
vouloir (*will*),	voulant,	voulu,	veux,	voulus.

INDEX

The Figure refers to the number of the Vocabulary in which the word
will be found.

THE END

Printed by R. & R. CLARK, *Edinburgh.*